Old Knives Tale

A MINERVA BIGGS MYSTERY

CORDELIA ROOK

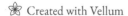

Chapter One

THE CLICHÉ HOLDS that small towns are full of old secrets. I understood this when I came to Bryd Hollow, but I probably would have understood it better if they'd said *old grudges* instead. The Towes held a grudge against the Gilroys. The Berks and the DeWitts held grudges against one another. Everybody held a grudge, if not two, against Keith Howell. (Keith Howell, for his part, had enough grudges to start his own small town.)

And then there was the Baird family grudge against me.

Well, not the entire Baird family. Percy was my friend. Which was funny, since he was the reason his mother and sister didn't like me, on account of that time I accidentally got him arrested for the murder of his father.

Which he didn't do, of course, and that all got cleared up—no small thanks to me. It wasn't easy, either. I think we can agree that getting shot demonstrates a certain amount of loyalty and commitment to making things right.

But no matter how intensely or how often Mrs. B insisted her staff were not servants, the fact was, they were definitely servants. And it seemed I'd violated a sacred servant code, in speaking to the police about the lord of the manor. I hadn't known my place.

They tried really hard not to be snobs, or at least they thought they did. But when you had that much money, it was pretty hard to avoid.

Which was why it was weird that Elaine Baird got engaged to a townie. And even weirder that she knocked on the door of the event planning office at Tybryd a few days after he proposed—looking for me.

Lots of people were knocking on the door that week, a circumstance I'd been warned to expect, Valentine's Day having been the weekend before. According to my boss Sajani, Valentine's, Christmas, and New Year's were the biggest days of the year for proposals. That meant a teeming horde of potential bridezillas, all desperate to get their weddings on Tybryd's ever-filling calendar.

A horde that was, apparently, to include Elaine Baird. Sajani's smile was silky as she got up to greet her. "Ms. Baird, how lovely to see you. I hear congratulations are in order."

With the tiniest of squeals, Elaine flapped her left hand. The ring was pretty modest, for a Baird. But probably really expensive for a veterinarian. "Yes they are!" she trilled. "That's why I'm here."

"Of course. Have a seat." Sajani waved gracefully at the chair in front of her desk, before moving with equal grace to the chair behind it. Desks and computers notwithstanding, the events office looked more like a parlor than an office (probably because it had once been a parlor), and Sajani, with her sophisticated updos and effortless poise, looked like she could have been born in it. I often felt clumsy by comparison. "Can I offer you some coffee? Sparkling water?"

"Um ..." Elaine looked over at my desk, where I was still sitting. I hadn't seen any reason to get up; our exchanges on her rare visits to Tybryd were mainly limited to polite greetings of three words or less. Not even Plant had gotten up from his rug in the corner. Just given one lazy thump of his tail when he heard the squeal, without even opening his eyes.

But it seemed I was to get more than three words today. "I was actually looking for Minerva." She gave me the hearty smile that was always a bit too reminiscent of her father's for my taste. "I probably should have called on my way over. Any chance you're available?"

"Of course she is!" Sajani said before I could answer. Behind Elaine's back, she gestured frantically at me, which was when I realized I probably looked like I'd been turned to stone. Or like an utter nitwit.

I stood and snapped my gaping mouth closed. Why on earth would she want to talk to me instead of Sajani? Not only did Elaine not like me, I was by far the junior member of the two-person events team. I'd been there less than four months.

There was one obvious answer to that question: Percy had made her do it. Bless his heart, he was one of the sweetest people I'd ever known, but he did, on occasion, cross over to the bossy side.

I tried not to cringe as I echoed Sajani's words. "Of course I am. Can *I* offer you something to drink?"

"No, no. I'm actually hoping not to stay long."

"Should we just grab a quick look at the calendar then, if you're in a hurry?"

"*We're* in a hurry," Elaine said. "The calendar can wait. I was really hoping your first official duty as my wedding planner could be to come with me to see Keith Howell. I have an appointment with him at eleven, but you know what he's like, or at least I assume you do, and he hates me. And I can't send Phil, because the whole point is to surprise Phil."

"Ah," I said. "So this is for Phil's dog?" Keith Howell had a number of very niche and not very lucrative careers, one of which was designing custom pet clothing. Gretchen occasionally displayed his samples in Noah's Bark, and Sajani had used him more than once to make dog and cat outfits to match a wedding party's. Honestly, the things brides—and mothers-in-law, and sometimes grooms—would ask for. Usually with a perfectly straight face.

"And his two cats," said Elaine. "I thought Graciela could have a bridesmaid's dress, and we could outfit the cats the same as the ring bearers. But I'd kind of rather you be there to do some of the talking." She gave me that Clifford Baird smile again. "I'll take you to the diner for fries after."

I couldn't help but laugh. The way she drew out the word *fries* made it clear that Percy had told her the

way to my heart. "No bribes necessary. I'd be happy to go."

Well, maybe *happy* wasn't the right word, considering Keith Howell was a known ratbag. But I was at least willing. I'd met him twice; he'd been unpleasant both times, and gotten my name wrong the second one. But as I understood it, that was practically affection, compared to how he treated everybody else.

"You don't mind if I leave Plant?" I asked Sajani. I usually didn't bring him to the office if I wasn't going to be there all day. "There's a bone in my top drawer if you need to go out."

Sajani assured me it was fine, and shooed me out the door. A few minutes later I was sitting in the passenger seat of Elaine's SUV, steeped in an awkward silence that was about as excruciating as you'd expect.

Keith's house wasn't far (almost nothing in Bryd Hollow was), but it was too far to spend the whole ride like that. I decided to take a direct approach. "So. I take it Percy made you ask me to plan the wedding?"

Elaine laughed—not her father's grating fake chuckle, but a genuine laugh. It reminded me of Percy's laugh, actually. I relaxed a little. "Yes. Yes he did. He sat me and Mom down and gave us a *lecture.*"

"A lecture?" This was worse than I'd feared. "I'm so sorry. What about?"

Elaine turned south, toward a part of Bryd Hollow that had been affluent a hundred years before, but now looked worn down, bordering on shabby. "About how you guys have been hanging out, and he likes you a lot, and it's time we stopped acting like children and started

showing you the respect and courtesy somebody who took a bullet for him deserves."

She glanced at me, then frowned. The latter was probably brought on by the proximity of my jaw to my lap. "What part of that tripped you up?"

It was the *likes you a lot* part, but I wasn't about to say so. I wasn't an eighth-grader. At least not on the outside.

Percy and I did hang out a lot, that was true. But I was pretty sure our friendship had reached that point where it had gone on too long to become anything more. He was nothing if not a gentleman, and I was nothing if not a bumbling nitwit, and so neither of us made a move until I guessed it was too late to make one.

If either of us had even wanted to make one in the first place. Percy *had* kissed me once—on the top of the head. While I lay in the hospital. As he was saying good-bye. I was pretty sure that didn't qualify as having intentions.

For my part, I went back and forth on the idea. There was no denying that Percy was adorable. That cliché about a smile lighting up a room? It could've been coined with him in mind. And he employed that smile often. Nobody could make me laugh like Percy could.

But us as a couple was not a very practical idea. He was a gazillionaire in charge of a great American dynasty's estate. I was more like a dollarfiftyaire, in charge of making sure the hot appetizers were served on schedule. He definitely ran at a different speed than I did.

And in very different circles. World travel, formal occasions, assorted rich-people stuff. Just last month the

internet had practically exploded with a picture of him and a famous actress. He said he didn't even know her, that he'd just been standing next to her at a charity thing. But even so. Nobody was being greeted by a picture of me with some celebrity every time they opened their browser.

Percy might have been adorable, but that didn't mean I wanted his life. Or that I could fit into it.

Plus, I suspected Plant was the one he really liked (a feeling Plant returned tenfold). There was always the possibility he was using me to get to my dog.

But like I said, I had no intention of telling Elaine all —or any—of that. I instead mumbled something about sometimes having a reaction to that whole taking a bullet thing.

Elaine looked at me again, her expression of sympathy sincere. "He told us that was the second time you'd been shot. And that the first one was bad."

"It was bad," I agreed. "But there's no need for him to make me the family charity case over it. If he feels guilty that I got shot last fall, he can let that go."

"I would not call it guilt," said Elaine, then kept talking, leaving me no opportunity to ask what she would call it. "Anyway it's not charity on *my* part. I wouldn't trust the biggest day of my life to you just as a favor to my brother, would I? And besides, Phil loves you."

"Phil loves Plant," I corrected. "Like I'm sure he loves all his patients."

Elaine's voice went so soft I barely recognized it. "Phil loves everybody. Even me." She seemed to catch herself sounding vulnerable, and fell back on her unfortunate—and probably unconscious—Clifford Baird impression. "The point is, I'm sure you'll do a great job."

"I appreciate the vote of confidence. I'll certainly try."

She pulled over to the side of the road, then grinned at me as she put the car in park. "Great. You can start now."

The assignment gave me no pause. It didn't sound like too great a challenge, talking to a guy about pet clothes. I mean sure, I knew Keith Howell was a crank, and that the meeting would probably be the lowlight of my day. But in the grand scheme of things, how bad could it be, really?

Well. Bad.

Chapter Two

THE PREVIOUS TWO occasions on which I'd met Keith Howell were at the event planning office; I'd never seen his house before. It stood out as especially dilapidated, probably enough so to annoy his neighbors. The yard was choked with weeds, and the brick steps leading up to his peeling front door were crumbling.

Our knock was answered by the most horrendous squawking imaginable. This turned out to be Keith's cockatiel, whom I met as soon as I stepped across the threshold, when he swooped down and bit the top of my head. I was pretty sure he came away with a little bit of hair. I hadn't even realized biting was a thing cockatiels did.

"Buckingham!" Keith waved the bird off with a gravelly declaration that we were clients, not guests. So it was perfectly acceptable, I guessed, for one's pets to bite guests?

Once the gray-feathered assailant was out of my face (he moved on to eyeing us moodily from the nearby bannister), I saw that Keith hadn't bothered to change out of his slippers for the occasion, though he was wearing jeans and a t-shirt, at least. He was a greasy-haired, sour-faced man who immediately brought to mind Ebenezer Scrooge, and in true Scrooge fashion, he dismissed our greetings with, "Well I wasn't about to turn down business in these lean times, was I? Even if it is for a Baird."

"Not a Baird for long!" Elaine gave him her very fakest smile, the one that always made me feel she had an abnormal amount of gums. "And I know you and Buckingham and Suffolk all want the best for Phil's big day."

Having met Buckingham, I was a little afraid to find out who Suffolk was, but I plucked up my courage and followed Keith through the tragically furnished living room (so much conflicting plaid) and into the kitchen. As we walked, Elaine leaned over to whisper in my ear. "Really lean into how happy this will make Phil. He might be the only human Keith actually likes."

The whispering was unnecessary, since Buckingham had taken to squawking again. At least he didn't attack me as he flew past us to perch on the back of an enormous gray cat lazing on the kitchen table. Suffolk, I presumed.

Elaine and I sat, though we hadn't been specifically invited to do so. "So, Buckingham and Suffolk," I said brightly. "Do you have a particular fondness for old English dukedoms?"

Keith allowed that he did, but before he could elaborate (something he seemed downright eager to do, for such a dour man), Suffolk hissed and pounced, narrowly missing my face with a swipe of his paw, but catching the hand I threw up to defend myself.

"Odsbodikins!" I jumped out of my chair, shaking my injured hand.

With another screech, the displaced Buckingham went to perch on top of the fridge, while Suffolk jumped to the floor and flounced from the room in high dudgeon. Like he was the injured party here. Just what these Howell animals had against me, I could not fathom, but I was both glad and sorry that Plant wasn't with me.

"Do you mind if I rinse my hand in the sink?" I asked, maybe a little too pointedly, when Keith failed to apologize for the (second, if we were keeping score, which I was) assault on my person.

"Go on then," he said. "But you can't blame Suffolk, you know. He's only protecting his house from robbers and ne'er-do-wells."

Had he seriously just said *ne'er-do-wells*? Honestly, the man might have been rehearsing for a play. *Casting call: town crank. Resemblance to Scrooge a plus.*

"But we're neither of those things," Elaine pointed out, while I washed the scratch with cold water.

"Suffolk seems to differ with you on that," said Keith. "Least where Moira here is concerned."

"Minerva," I corrected.

"Whatever. He's got to be on high alert these days. Someone broke in here, and I know they'll be back. Suffolk knows it, too."

"Oh? What happened?" I asked as I rejoined them at the table.

Keith scoffed. "Nothing the so-called police care about, I'll tell you that much. Tried to file a report, but Roark wasn't even writing it all down. He's useless."

"Oh my gosh!" said Elaine. "I hope you weren't hurt."

"Wasn't home." Keith scowled at her. "Why would someone break in while I was home to catch them at it? This was on Sunday. I was at church."

"What was stolen?" I asked.

"Nothing, as far as I can tell."

I frowned. "But things were disturbed?"

Keith looked at me like I was the weird one. "Not that I could see."

"But then ... how do you know somebody broke in?" asked Elaine.

"Well if they didn't, they tried to," Keith said. "Buckingham started screaming bloody murder the second I got back. And Suffolk was *very* upset. *Very* suspicious of someone's intentions. He has a way of narrowing his eyes, when something isn't right, and he looked like that. Now, he couldn't be suspicious of someone unless someone was there for him to be suspicious of, could he?" He leaned back and crossed his arms, as if he'd just scored an incontrovertible point.

So his evidence was that a bird was squawking and a cat was making dubious faces—things birds and cats did with some regularity. And these particular two more than most, I suspected. I began to see why Officer Roark had treated this matter as less than urgent.

Besides, in my admittedly brief experience with Keith Howell's home, I could not think what anybody could possibly want to steal from him. Against my better judgment, I indulged my curiosity by asking him who he thought might have a reason to break into his house.

"All sorts of people," Keith said. "Ollie Gilroy, for sure. Or one of them Digbys." He narrowed his eyes at Elaine. "Maybe even one of your ilk. I'll bet I've got some old things the Bairds would be interested in."

No doubt seeing her opportunity to get to business, Elaine beamed at him. "I promise, the only thing I want from you is your help giving Phil a wonderful wedding day. I'm hoping to surprise him by having roles for Graciela and Jem and Scout. And of course they'll need to be dressed for it, and you're the only one I would trust for that."

Keith allowed himself to be led to the more lucrative subject, and we spent half an hour—during which he did not offer us so much as a glass of water—discussing outfits and colors and timelines. (Elaine said she was aiming for a spring wedding, which I found a tad alarming, considering Tybryd weddings were generally booked at least a year ahead.) Despite his less-than-ideal attitude, there was never any question Keith was going to accept the work.

"Best have Melanie be my point of contact, though," he said, jerking his chin at me.

"Minerva," I corrected. Again.

"Whatever. I'm sure Elaine fancies herself a globetrotter. You're probably the easier one to get a hold of."

"Absolutely. The details are my job." I reached into my purse for a business card. "I'll leave this with you."

Keith accompanied us to the door, and spent several

seconds after we walked away standing on the porch, peering suspiciously at the unkempt shrubs as if he expected his would-be thief to leap out of them.

As promised, Elaine and I went to Deirdre's for lunch, and easily banished the dark cloud that was Keith Howell with the sunny sounds of oldies streaming from the speakers lining Honor Avenue, and the might of pimento cheese fries.

A little nervously, I brought up the fact that a spring event at Tybryd might be an issue, unless she meant two springs from now.

But Elaine just smiled. "That's what I'm hoping, honestly. I actually don't particularly want to get married there. I mean, who wants to get married at the office, right?"

She laughed at her own joke, so I joined in to be polite, even though Tybryd really wasn't her office. As they'd divvied up the responsibilities of the family business, the resort became Percy's domain, while Elaine tended to its ancillary lines of spa products, specialty foods, and wine. These days, when she wasn't traveling, she worked almost exclusively out of her home office at Baird House. We barely saw her.

"Personally, I'd rather get married at the house," she went on. "But Phil's mother would throw a fit if I didn't at least check on Tybryd first. You know how Bryd Hollow people can be."

I nodded, my mouth being too full of cheese to answer. I'd quickly learned that holding their weddings (and anniversaries, and sometimes milestone birthdays) at Tybryd was more than just the dream of every Bryd

Hollow citizen; as far as they were concerned, it was their absolute right. I'd already been railed at by more than one person who insisted locals should be given heavy discounts.

"I still want you to plan it either way," Elaine said. "If we can't do it at Tybryd, you can just do it on the side as a contract job." She took a thoughtful sip of her sweet tea, as if contemplating something that had just occurred to her for the first time. "Unless you don't *want* to."

"No, I do," I assured her. I was now fully on board with the hope that we wouldn't be able to get one of Tybryd's ballrooms or gardens for the occasion; a private side job would mean extra money, and keeping Plant in kibble and bones wasn't cheap.

All in all, I had fun at that lunch. I was firmly of the opinion that Phil Mendoza (and, to be frank about it, the removal of her father from her life, abrupt though that had been) had improved Elaine Baird. She wasn't so bad when she was relaxed and happy.

By the time she dropped me back off at Tybryd, I was feeling pretty good about this new life I'd carved out of these old mountains. It was cold and drizzly, and not the best light to view the estate in, but Tybryd was always beautiful. I smiled up at one of the gargoyles guarding the red roof, before walking inside to bask in the familiar scents of pine and woodsmoke. The lobby-slash-bar was grand and luxurious, my office down the main hall elegant and cozy.

I got to work in this building—this living, breathing piece of history—and bring my dog to the office almost every day. I didn't have a palatial apartment or anything, but I'd moved out of the one above Gretchen's pet store, and my new place on the east side of town was at least an upgrade from that. (It had four whole rooms, for one thing.)

And I had the best friends a girl could ask for. Percy and Snick, Paul and Carrie, Gretchen and Sajani. I was getting to know everybody else, too; Percy had dispelled the last vestiges of hesitation to trust a newcomer by being seen with me often.

All I'd wanted when I came to Bryd Hollow was to make a new home here, a real home. And I'd done it.

You're thinking I jinxed myself with all this smug self-satisfaction, and you would be right. Late that afternoon—almost five, in fact, when I ought to have been closing up the office—I was brought face to face with just how not-perfect my life was, in the person of Bonnie Digby. One of my least favorite Bryd Hollow residents, and I included Keith Howell in that assessment.

My day descended into the lowest of lowlight territory from there.

Chapter Three

ODSBODIKINS. Sajani was giving a tour to a heart surgeon who was scouting Tybryd for a convention, leaving nobody but me to deal with Bonnie Digby. I didn't know Bonnie well, but I knew her just well enough to understand that this was probably going to be the least fun part of my day.

We'd had an altercation once at Noah's Bark, starting with her demanding a refund for a plastic sandwich bag full of regurgitated cat food, and ending with her demanding my immediate termination. Fortunately, Gretchen couldn't stand her either, and I'd kept my job. Less fortunately, Bonnie had left the bag of cat puke behind on the counter when she left.

I'd never seen the woman with her before, but she looked enough like Bonnie to mark them as sisters, or at least close cousins. Which one was the prettier depended on how conventional you liked your beauty. They had the same beachy waves and blue eyes, but the sister had a much bigger nose, and a light scar at one temple, along her ear and partly hidden behind her hair, that might have been from a burn. I thought her face had more character than Bonnie's, which resembled a china doll's.

Not that I expected a lot of character from a Digby.

"Bonnie." I gave her as professional a smile as I could manage. "How nice to see you. How can I help?"

"Oh, it's ..." Bonnie tilted her head at me, brow furrowed, as if deciding just how disgruntled she wanted to be. "What again was your name?"

Plant chose that moment to emerge from under my desk, stretching and wagging his tail at the newcomers. He started wiggling toward them, but I saw the look on Bonnie's face and grabbed hold of his collar.

"*Ohmylordyoustillhavethatdevildog!*" She jumped back like she'd been attacked.

Devil dog? Okay, Plant was large. And black. And square-headed, and a tad jowly. I would allow he could look intimidating, to some. But *devil dog* seemed excessive. Particularly when he'd dropped into such a handsome sit at my command.

Bonnie's eyes flashed from Plant to me, having settled at maximum disgruntlement. "*Now* I remember. You're that wench from the pet store."

"Bonnie," her companion-and-probably-sister hissed.

Bonnie turned to her. "Just tell her to keep that dog away from me!"

"The dog isn't near you!" the woman said.

That was true, but I nevertheless told Plant to go to his rug, which he did, thankfully, in a perfectly gentlemanly manner. Bolstered to magnanimity by my dog's clearly superior behavior, I decided to ignore the use of the word *wench* and address the lesser of the evils before me. I held my hand out to the sister. "Minerva Biggs."

"Brooke Digby." Her handshake was firm and confident, and I noted expensive shoes and a designer handbag. I wondered whether she lived here in Bryd Hollow.

"Nice to meet you," I said.

"Likewise." She gave me a light grimace that suggested there might be a sense of humor in there somewhere. "I'm sorry for barging in without an appointment. To tell you the truth, Bonnie was going on and on and on about her wedding so much, our father begged us to get out of the house and go find some people who cared."

And you thought I would be one of them? I bit back the question before it could escape my mouth.

"We started out just window shopping," Brooke went on, oblivious to my inner rudeness. "You know, just getting some preliminary ideas of the kind of wedding she might want. But we finished at the dress shop earlier than we expected—mostly because we didn't have an appointment there either—so we figured we'd just swing by here and see if anyone was available."

"Sure. So you're ... engaged?" I addressed the latter to Bonnie, trying not to look offensively surprised.

Bonnie waggled her hand, much like Elaine had done a few hours earlier. Her ring was somewhat less tasteful—the stone was gigantic to the point of garishness. It was also pink. "Yes, are you the only event planner we can pick?"

Brooke gave her an exasperated look. "Bonnie, really?"

"There are two of us," I said. "But since I'm the only one here right now, why don't we just take a look at the basics, like dates? If you decide to move forward, we can discuss Sajani working your event instead, if you'd prefer." *I know I would.*

"Oh, I'll definitely be moving forward," said Bonnie.

"This would just be for the ceremony?" I asked. Assuming the mutual father Brooke referred to was Ron Digby, Bonnie's family owned Rapunzel's, the only fine-dining restaurant in town and one of the best in the state. Its reputation was grander than ever, thanks to the recent acquisition of a celebrity chef. It was the obvious choice for her reception.

But Bonnie shook her head. "Ceremony, reception, the whole works." She sat down (uninvited, but since that was poor form on my part, I couldn't really fault her for it) and started rummaging through her purse. "I've been dreaming of a Tybryd wedding my whole life, and I am absolutely one hundred percent getting married here. I have some sketches I did, like *years* ago, just give me a sec to find the book."

Of course she had sketches. She was exactly the type who would have sketches. Probably drawn when she was twelve.

Because of course she'd been planning this her whole life. And yet she'd waltzed in here without an appointment, probably multiple days after she'd gotten engaged, as an afterthought at the end of a shopping trip. Just expecting us to be able to accommodate her. No rush to get it on the calendar or anything. It was only Tybryd.

"All right." I pulled over a chair for Brooke, then sat

behind my keyboard and woke up my computer. "Did you have a timeframe in mind?"

"Next month would be good," said Bonnie.

I willed myself not to laugh in her face. Or to look at all pleased to be able to disappoint her. But I'll tell you, neither was easy. "I'm sorry, that won't be possible."

"What are you talking about?" she asked. "Next month is *March*. That's not a big wedding month."

"We're booking at least a year out right now, even for the off-peak months."

"A *year*? That is *bull*." Bonnie stood and jabbed a finger at me. "You just don't want townies littering the place up, is that it? Or is it me in particular you're out to get?"

"Bonnie." Brooke took her sister's elbow, trying to tug her back down to her chair.

"What?" Bonnie glared at her. "Nobody is getting in my way, least of all a lady who tried to cheat me out of the price of cat food."

"Calm down, Bonbon." Brooke sounded exactly like a mother trying to soothe a toddler's tantrum. "Nobody is out to get you."

"I did not try to ... that is not what ..." I sputtered, then stopped. Was I really going to try to defend my part in the cat puke incident? Did that really require defending? That way lay madness, surely. "I'm afraid I have no special power over the calendar. We can do a lot here at Tybryd, but we can't actually create time."

Brooke chuckled at the joke, but Bonnie was having none of it. "I bet you guys are making time for *Elaine*."

"Nope," I said, glad I could say it honestly. "Elaine is subject to the laws of physics, just like everybody else."

Bonnie leaned over my desk. "I want to see that calendar."

I had to grip the top of my monitor to keep her from turning it around. "I'm sorry, but that's private information."

"Made-up information, you mean."

"Okay, that's enough." Brooke's voice was firm, but she patted her sister's arm, still the gentle peacemaker. "I know this is disappointing, Bonbon, but you have to look at it from their side. A lot of places book this far out. Rapunzel's gets booked way far ahead, too, you know that. If you still want to get married here, you can. And if you don't want to wait, we can go somewhere else. It's still all up to you."

Please don't want to wait, I silently begged Bonnie. *Please go somewhere else.*

No such luck. The most Bonnie would do was table the issue of a date for the time being, until she could speak with my supervisor about it. In the meanwhile, she produced the promised ancient and battered notebook. In it were several sketches of what appeared to be doves around a gazebo, with a stick-figure bride and a stick-figure groom at the center.

I cocked my head at the cloud-shaped blobs at the edges. "Are those ... sheep?"

"Yeah, I definitely want sheep. Preferably with their coats dyed in the wedding colors, which will be lilac and pumpkin. You know, like a spring and fall theme. I was thinking we could do the boy sheep pumpkin, and the girls lilac. Or should we maybe go by size?"

The conversation didn't improve from there. It seemed the sheep were required accessories for her Bo-Peep style wedding dress, but the idea was for them to double as a sort of petting zoo for the guests. I mumbled something about livestock permits (I had no idea whether it had any basis in truth), and suggested tabling that issue as well, before moving on to the wedding colors she'd mentioned. Both Brooke and I tried to encourage her toward *either* lilac *or* pumpkin—in Brooke's case, probably out of abject terror of having to wear some combination of the two—but Bonnie was determined that both have equal representation, including alternating the table settings.

By the time she got around to a dedicated security team for ejecting any guest wearing white, cream, or ivory, I was extremely grateful to hear my phone's ringtone.

Even better: Ruby Walker's name came up on the display. Normally I would not be excited about a call from the police, but it suited this occasion perfectly; the police had the benefit of requiring a person to answer them.

"I'm so sorry, I have to get this, it looks like an emergency," I said to Bonnie and Brooke, tapping my phone at the same time. "Ruby, hi, what can I do for you?"

"Do you know where Keith Howell's house is?" she asked.

Keith Howell? Odsbodikins, had the man filed a

complaint against me for upsetting his cat, or something? "Humility Lane, right? I was just there."

"When?"

"Before lunch. Elaine Baird and I went to see him about her wedding."

"That would explain your business card on his kitchen table. Can you come back? Alone, and now, or thereabouts."

"I ..." One glance at the Digby sisters made up my mind on that point. Whatever this was about, it could not possibly be worse than what I was doing. "Yeah. Sure."

"Great. Oh, and you aren't squeamish, are you?"

Now there was a question you didn't necessarily want to be asked by a police officer. "About some things, I guess, but I wouldn't say I'm *especially* squeamish. Why?"

She didn't answer. Definitely a bad sign. "Good enough. When I said alone, I meant that if you've got Plant with you, you need to leave him off at home first."

Then again, maybe it *could* be worse than what I was doing. I swallowed against the not-good feeling that was rising in my throat, and repeated the question of why. This time she answered—sort of—but it did nothing to ease my mind.

"Because your dog is a giant oaf, and I don't want him trampling up my crime scene."

Chapter Four

IT SEEMED to me that the word *squeamish* in juxtaposition with the phrase *crime scene* could only mean that Keith Howell was either badly hurt or (more likely) dead.

Which was what I told the Digby sisters while I grabbed my coat and Plant's leash, and shooed them out of the office. Brooke looked dismayed. Bonnie just shrugged and said, "Good riddance to bad rubbish, if you ask me," before extracting a promise that I would drop some samples at her house the following day, to be returned when she got a "real" appointment with Sajani.

When they'd been dispensed with, I took Plant for the shortest walk I could get away with, and dropped him at my apartment with a nice bone. Then I freaked out all the way to Keith's house.

Was I a suspect, because of the business card? Probably not, or at least that probably wasn't the main reason for Ruby's call. I was pretty sure summoning the suspects to the scene of the crime was not how policing worked.

So what could she want with me that required my presence there? That required me not to be *squeamish*, no less?

Odsbodikins. I'll be honest, I was feeling pretty squeamish.

An animal control van was pulling away just as I pulled up, giving me an unpleasant sinking feeling that did nothing for my anxious stomach. I'd had a bit of a mishap the autumn before, for which poor Plant had paid the price. Just the thought of it made my hands shake a little.

I guessed it was Buckingham and Suffolk's turn, now. My stomach rolled again as I thought about how scared and confused they must be. However ornery they were with intruders, I was sure they loved Keith. He certainly loved them.

Two police cars were parked out front, along with a marked car designating it as the county medical examiner's. A uniformed policeman was on the front walkway, holding a bunch of yellow police tape and talking to an older couple I didn't recognize.

"... cat is *always* in our garden," the woman was saying as I approached. "The bird was even with it once! So when Ollie saw the door wide open and the cat on the porch, of course he went inside. Who *wouldn't* want to have a word with Keith about his carelessness? Only it turned out he wasn't careless so much as he was dead. This time."

"Officer Roark," I said, and stopped there. What else could I say? *Hello* seemed too breezy for what was clearly a serious situation, and *hi* and *hey* were even worse in that regard. *Nice to see you* was right out, what with crime scenes generally not being nice places. I nodded at the couple, who were now goggling at me in silence. The man in particular looked shaken.

A little furrow appeared between Roark's brows. Maybe I'd screwed up my greeting, after all. Or maybe he couldn't place me. It was getting dark, and I'd only met the lanky, auburn-haired young officer a couple of times before. Mostly when I was at the police station arguing with Ruby.

"I'm Minerva," I offered. "Ruby called me."

Roark gave me a shy smile. "I know who you are. You can go on in, but call out to let her know you're here, then wait in the foyer for her. You don't want to go upstairs. You'll find gloves and shoe covers on the bottom step."

"Thank you." That also felt like an odd thing to say. Was I really grateful to be walking into ... whatever I was walking into?

I stopped just inside the open front door, but I couldn't help but glance around. Apart from the lack of guardian birds, things were just as they'd been earlier, unfortunate plaids and all. "Ruby?" I called up the staircase.

"On my way!" she called down. "Stay down there."

That was not going to be a problem; whatever she and Roark didn't want me to see, I was pretty sure I agreed with them. I hugged myself, rubbing my forearms in an attempt to get warm. I heard Ruby exchange a few words with somebody I couldn't see.

"Put some of those gloves on, if you don't mind," she

said as she came down the stairs. She was carrying a plastic evidence bag, but it was opaque white rather than clear, and I couldn't see what was inside.

I reached into the box (on the bottom step, as promised) for a pair of gloves. "Do I need the shoe covers, too?"

Ruby glanced around, then flicked the nearest switch. Bright light filled the foyer from a fixture over-head. "No, this will work. You won't have to move from where you're standing now. Sorry to call you to some-thing like this."

"Something like what, if you don't mind my asking? You didn't specify exactly on the phone."

"Keith's been killed. No question it's murder. Mean-while, Basil closed Yore and went to the Virgin Islands for a week." Ruby pursed her lips. I couldn't tell whether it was Keith's murder she disapproved of, or Basil's vaca-tion. "Since you're a history nut, I thought you might be the next best thing."

Yore was the local antique shop, Basil its owner. And in his absence, Ruby needed a history nut? I'll admit I was intrigued, despite the announcement that there was a corpse upstairs (which hadn't come as a shock, all things considered). "What happened?" I asked.

"Someone put the handle of a knife through his eye."

I frowned. "If they had a knife, wouldn't it have been easier to stab him with the sharp end?"

"For that matter, it would've been easier to stab him with an entirely different knife," said Ruby. "This one is not sharp, and it is not your usual knife. It looks old, which is why I wanted to ask you about it."

While I got progressively less eager, Ruby reached her gloved hand into the evidence bag (bad), pulled out this unusual murder weapon (worse), and held it up for my inspection (worst).

For a second or two I only squinted at it, in no hurry to discover just how squeamish I might turn out to be. Then I opened my eyes wider. And wider again.

Then I downright gaped.

The blood on the handle was forgotten as I stared at the blade—and what was engraved on it. "That's a notation knife!"

"Never heard of it," Ruby said. "But it's old, right?"

I leaned in closer. "Can you ..." I made a little twirling motion with my finger, asking Ruby to turn the knife so I could get a better look. Excited as I was by what I was pretty sure I was looking at, I had no interest in actually touching something that had until so recently been in Keith Howell's eye.

Ruby dutifully tilted it up, then turned it over to give me a view of the other side. I guessed it made sense that the murderer had used the handle, since it was narrower than the blade. The latter was wide and blocky, straight on the top and curved on the bottom, coming to a delicate point. It was discolored with age.

And the flat of it was engraved with musical notation. Lines, notes, the whole works, like reading sheet music. Except the kind that had just killed a guy.

What in all blazes was a notation knife doing in Bryd Hollow?

Well, killing a guy. But besides that.

"If it's real, then yes, it's very old. Like, sixteenth-century old." I shook my head, a little deflated, and straightened back up again. "But it can't be. Real, I mean."

"How do you know?" Ruby asked.

"I guess I don't. You'd have to find an expert at authenticating this sort of thing to tell you for sure. But notation knives are rare."

"How rare?"

"Very. Extremely. If that were real, it would probably be priceless. It's not the kind of thing you would use to kill somebody, and it's definitely not the kind of thing you would leave behind after."

Ruby shrugged. "The killer may not have known how valuable it is."

"It's also not the kind of thing you'd just have lying around handy. I can't imagine owning one and *not* knowing how valuable it is. You'd have to be a collector of some kind." I cast a pointed look to my right, where the foyer opened up to the living room—the worn furniture, the stained carpet. "The super rich kind."

"A family heirloom, maybe? Used to make a point?"

"But notation knives aren't just antiques," I said, "they're *artifacts*. And even if one of these old families somehow did have one that was passed down through the generations, I can't imagine the killer just leaving it here."

"Do you by chance recognize the notes?"

"No, I can't read music." I cocked my head as Ruby returned the knife to its bag. "It's weird, though, I think the lyrics are usually engraved along with the music."

"So if it's fake, maybe that's something the counterfeiter got wrong."

"Either that, or it's an especially unusual knife among unusual knives. Anyway, they're most likely songs of thanks for the food. One on the front, one on the back, for before and after the meal. I think. I should mention that I haven't read up on these lately, so I couldn't swear to anything I'm telling you."

"All right then, thank you," said Ruby. "And what time were you and Elaine here earlier?"

"We got here at eleven. I don't know the exact time we left, but I doubt we were even here an hour. We were talking about outfits Elaine wanted made for Phil's pets, as a wedding surprise." I tugged at one of the gloves. "Is it okay to take these off?"

"Long as you don't touch anything. And what about the rest of the day, between say one and five?"

"Where was I, you mean?"

"No, I was hoping you could tell me where I was." Ruby lowered her head and looked at me over the top of her teal-framed glasses, a signature move that suggested I was a bit slow. "Yes, you."

I'd been so distracted by the knife, I'd almost forgotten that I was one of the last people to see the victim alive. "I've got people who can attest to my whereabouts for pretty much the whole day."

"Good, you can give that information to Roark on your way out. I take it you didn't see anyone else here, besides Keith?"

"Only his cat and bird. But he was jumpy. Actually, all three of them were jumpy. He told us somebody had been trying to break in." I got the gloves off and then, unsure what to do with them, stuffed them in my pockets. "I guess he wasn't crazy, huh?"

Ruby took the glasses all the way off this time. "What on the lord's earth gave you the impression Keith Howell wasn't crazy?"

I blinked at her, feeling a bit like the question was a trap. Wasn't it obvious? "Well, because somebody really did break in, like he said."

Ruby snorted. "In the time I've worked for the great town of Bryd Hollow, Keith Howell has reported some crime or other more weeks than he hasn't. Somebody is always out to get him."

"But obviously somebody really was out to get him."

"Somebody was today," she agreed. "But that doesn't mean there was a break-in three days ago. We don't know that it's related."

That struck me as frankly ridiculous. Maybe Ruby didn't *want* it to be related. Maybe she felt guilty, because her officer had dismissed Keith's report. Despite her having put the glasses back on—a clear indication that she was done with me—I crossed my arms. "I guess you can't be completely *sure*, no, but you're looking into it, right? You don't think it's a suspicious coincidence?"

I could tell by the way her chest moved that Ruby most definitely muffled a sigh. "Obviously we will look into it. But speculation is pointless until we've finished processing the scene. Which, much as I appreciate your input, I need to get back to now."

She put a hand on my shoulder and turned me around to face the door. "Thanks again, Minerva."

Well alrighty, then. I guessed the chief of police with

decades of experience didn't feel she needed a young event planner to tell her how to do her job. Weird.

But not as weird as a notation knife showing up in Keith Howell's house.

It couldn't be real.

Could it?

Chapter Five

BALANCING two paper cups and a matching paper bag in his hands, Percy was obliged to use his foot to close the office door behind him. It didn't cross my mind to get up and help him until it was too late; I was too busy admiring his shoulders in that suit he was wearing. And his hands on the cups. It had never occurred to me before I met him to assign quality to hands, but Percy Baird had very nice hands.

He flashed me the dimples. Presumably just to torture me further. "Morning, Mini Bigs."

I narrowed my eyes at him, although I was somewhat placated by the likelihood that one of those cups was for me. "I thought we agreed to let the Mini Bigs thing die."

"We agreed to no such th—" He stopped abruptly and stared around, as if he couldn't entirely believe is eyes. "Where is my boy?"

"*My* boy is at home for the morning. I'll grab him on my way back." I sure as blazes didn't want to bring him along where I was going.

"Back from where?" Percy asked.

I bit my lip. "I was kind of hoping to play a little hooky. I don't think Sajani will mind. I'll stay late to make up for it."

"Sajani's cool, but make sure the big boss doesn't find out." He gave me an exaggerated grimace. "I hear he's a real jerk."

"Aw, he's not so bad. Especially when he brings me stuff."

He set the cups down on my desk, and handed me the bag. "Earl Grey and a mini lemon donut."

"My hero. Thank you." I raised a brow at him. "Mini, though? What are you suggesting?"

"That they were out of full-sized, Twig."

I huffed. Tony at Deirdre's diner called me Twig, and Percy knew I hated it. "That is not better than Mini Bigs."

"Mini Bigs, preferred nickname. Got it." Laughing, he ducked to avoid the napkin I tossed at him. "Sajani's not here?"

"She's setting up a family reunion at the little inn." The little inn was one of many separate buildings scattered throughout the grounds, some old, some constructed in the years since Tybryd became a resort. Boasting almost thirty guest rooms and its own kitchen, restaurant, and bar, it wasn't actually all that little. But it did offer a cozier atmosphere for groups looking for something more private.

Percy picked one of the cups back up. "Good, I forgot to get something for her, and I didn't want to have to give her my tea."

I took a bite of the donut, closing my eyes in appreciation of the just-tart-enough lemon curd. The Seven Ravens in Bryd Hollow was more coffee shop than bakery, but they made the best donuts anywhere. "Well, I'm very grateful that you remembered me."

"Always. So what's the truancy about?"

"It's not *all* truancy, if that makes it sound any better. I do have to drop something off at a potential client's house. But I'd really like to go visit Suffolk and Buckingham after."

He blinked at me. "And those would be ... places in England?"

"They would be a cat and a cockatiel. County Animal Control has them."

"Ah." Percy gave me a sympathetic look. "Keith's?"

"You heard about Keith?"

"Saw Carrie on my way in."

As Tybryd's HR director, my friend Carrie had an office just down the hall from Percy's. Much as I loved it here in the hotel proper, I sometimes envied them their quaint executive building beyond the hedge maze. It was almost original to the estate, having begun life as a guest house. "So I guess Carrie heard it from Paul?" I asked.

"Obviously."

I laughed. Paul was Carrie's husband, my high-school sweetheart—and the town gossip. Or at least, he was tied with Snick for the latter position. "And Paul heard it from ..."

"Roark. Paul ran into him at Cullen's last night."

I leaned back in my chair. "Hm, so let me see if I can put all this together. You went to the office, heard this from Carrie, then went back out again"—I held up my cup to emphasize the Seven Ravens logo—"all the way into town, for tea and a donut? When there's a cafe right here in the lobby?"

Percy stuffed his hands into his pockets and rocked back on his heels, ostensibly to study his shoes. "I just wanted to check you're okay."

Sometimes it was really hard not to just throw caution to the wind and kiss him. He knew perfectly well that the Seven Ravens donuts were my favorite. "Thank you. I am okay." I gave him a sheepish look. "I'm actually a little ashamed of how okay I am."

"Why would you be ashamed?"

"A man is *dead*."

Percy's lips twitched. "Well, yeah, but it's Keith Howell."

I wadded up another napkin and threw it at him, but it fell harmlessly to my desk before it got anywhere near him. "Now you should be ashamed."

"Making macabre jokes is a time-honored way of dealing with grief."

"So you're grieving for Keith Howell?"

"Kind of. In the sense that I don't love it when anybody gets murdered."

I plucked at the edges of the fallen napkin. "Me neither, but to be brutally honest, I'm more curious about that knife than I am sad about Keith. Hence the guilt. Did Carrie tell you about the knife?"

"Only in the context of it being why Ruby called you. She said it was some kind of musical antique, which didn't sound right." Percy widened his eyes in faux fascination. "Did it sing? Was it a *magic* knife?"

"It was a notation knife. Here." I pulled out my phone and opened the browser, which immediately loaded the last page I'd looked at: a selection of images of notation knives. While he scrolled through them, I told him what I'd already told Ruby about the knives and their purpose.

"Oh ... kay," Percy said, still looking at the pictures. "That's weird."

"*Super* weird. I'm assuming it's counterfeit, right? I mean it can't be real. But even so. It's a very curious choice for a murder weapon."

"So it is." He handed my phone back. "And how does all this come back to Cambridge and Oxford?"

"Suffolk and Buckingham. I was thinking about them last night, almost as much as I was thinking about the knife. Nobody liked Keith, right?"

"Definitely not."

"So nobody is going to be looking out for them, or coming to claim them, and—"

"I'm sure Alan will," Percy cut in. "Eventually, anyway."

"Who's Alan?"

"Keith's son. I doubt Denise—that's Keith's ex-wife —will come out here, but Alan would have to, right? I think he lives on the west coast, though. And as far as I recall he's an even bigger jerk than Keith was. So I'm not sure how quickly he'll get around to worrying about the pets."

"Exactly my point! *Nobody* is worrying about them."

"Other than you, you mean."

I flung a hand at him. "Which is why I have to! It's not their fault that they were raised by somebody mean, who made them mean, too. And they're bound to be freaking out. It broke my heart when Plant was stuck at the shelter overnight, and this is so much worse. What if they actually saw Keith get killed?"

"I see," said Percy, although I wasn't entirely sure he did. His grave expression was looking like it required some effort to maintain. "You're thinking the bird is traumatized?"

"At the least! Knowing Buckingham as I now do, he could very well have had an altercation with the murderer! Anyway, I'm sure the people who work at the shelter are lovely, but they have a lot to do, and Suffolk and Buckingham are not going to be the easiest to be nice to. Somebody should give them a little special attention. Not that they'll be glad it's me."

"The shelter people won't be glad?"

"No, Suffolk and Buckingham won't be glad."

Percy's brow furrowed, as if that was anything like the weirdest thing I'd said. "Why wouldn't they be glad?"

"They hate me." I held up my scratched hand as proof of Suffolk's ill regard.

"It sounds like they hate everybody, though."

"I do get that sense," I agreed. "I'd still like to check on them, at least, and make sure they're okay."

Choosing to interpret Percy's nod as a blessing from Tybryd's supreme overlord, I straightened in my chair, scribbling a note for Sajani. "I'll stop by Bonnie Digby's on the way, so like I said, I won't be totally neglecting my duties."

"Bonnie Digby is the potential client?"

"Yep. She got engaged over Valentine's Day weekend, same as Elaine."

Percy's puff of laughter suggested he knew Bonnie, and was as surprised as I was that anybody had committed to a lifetime with her. "Engaged to whom? I didn't even know she was dating anybody."

"I don't know, actually. It was just her sister with her yesterday, and the meeting got cut short before we got around to minor details like the groom." I rummaged through the bag I'd put together for Bonnie, making sure everything I'd promised her was inside. I didn't even want to think about the tantrum she would throw if I forgot something.

"Her sister?" Percy asked. "Brooke's in town?"

"Brooke, yeah." Linen samples in both pumpkin and lilac, plus every available flavor of the signature chocolates we made on the premises. She was considering the latter for favors, provided they could be molded into the shape of sheep.

"We'd better get a move on, then," he said. "I have a couple of conference calls later that I can't miss. Plus you left Plant waiting."

I cocked my head at him. "You're coming with me? Don't you have bigger and better things to do, Mr. Hotel Tycoon?"

"Than visit a bird? How could I?" Percy held up my coat to help me into it, like it was 1952. I knew from experience that this did not make me special; he did it for all women. I'd long since decided it was more sweet than sexist. "I'm driving, though," he said.

"What, you object to my wreck?"

"I object to your driving."

I looked back over my shoulder at him. "What's wrong with my driving?"

He smiled, and I steadfastly did not stare at his dimples. "You drive like a grandma. We'd never get back in time."

As Percy's old Jeep was much nicer than my car, I voiced no objection. Besides, if pressed, I would have been forced to admit that I did drive a *little* like a grandma.

We started out talking about Elaine and Phil on the way into town, but that skirted too close to their wedding for my comfort. I didn't want Percy to know that I knew that he'd forced his sister to hire me. Or that I knew he'd given his family strict instructions to be nice to me.

Instead, I changed the subject to Keith. "Who would want to kill him, do you think?"

Percy shrugged one shoulder. "Pretty much everybody. Every one of his neighbors hated him, for starters."

"Yeah, I don't know who it was talking to Roark on the front lawn, but it sounded like the guy was the one who found the body, and his wife didn't sound too broken up about it, that's for sure. Apparently Suffolk is not their favorite."

"Suffolk is the cat, right? Or is that Buckingham?"

"Suffolk is the cat. But now that you mention it, I don't think they like Buckingham much, either."

"That was probably the Gilroys. They're his closest neighbors." Percy, who was rarely still, started tapping out a rhythm on the steering wheel. I turned my head to look out the window, because staring at your friend's hands—or anybody's hands, really—is weird.

"Anyway," I said, "pets aside, I can't imagine Keith was much fun to live with, if he was always imagining crimes and offenses against him."

"He's filed dozens of complaints over the years," Percy said. "And for the stupidest stuff you can imagine. Like, say a squirrel dropped some seed from a neighbor's bird feeder onto his lawn. He'd argue that since it originated in their yard, they should have to clean it up."

I laughed. "That is not a real example."

"It could be." He pulled onto Prudence Street, despite not having asked for directions. I guessed it wasn't surprising that he would know where to go. Bonnie had mentioned that she'd moved back in with her parents, and Ron Digby definitely qualified as a prominent citizen. This was the fanciest street in Bryd Hollow, home to anybody who was well off but did not bear the last name of Baird.

"It's number eighty-three," I offered, just in case.

Percy nodded. "And really, it's not only Keith himself. If you're looking for motive, it just depends how far back you want to go." He pointed at the Digby house as he parked on the street in front of it. "Right here, for example. The Howells have a long-standing feud with the Digbys."

"Really?" I considered the house, which was big, brick, and well maintained, including the spacious and manicured lawn. It was something of a contrast to Keith Howell's. I remembered Keith mentioning the Digbys among his suspects the day before (along with the Gilroys, and the Bairds for that matter), but I couldn't imagine they'd actually run into each other much. "About what?"

"I don't know. I'm not sure anybody knows. When I say long-standing, I mean *long*-standing, like over a century."

"I'm just dropping these off, you know," I said when Percy unbuckled his seatbelt. "Like, ring and run. I won't be a minute."

"Yeah, I just thought I'd say hi, congratulate Bonnie." He gave me a pointed look. "Find out who the lucky guy is, since you so thoroughly failed at small-town gossip."

"Hey, if you think small-town gossip is worth an encounter with Bonnie Digby, knock yourself out."

A curtain in the front window twitched as we approached the porch steps, and a fluffy white cat appeared, peering out at us with a slow swish of his tail. Male, judging by the size of him. He could've given Plant a run for his money in the big-head department.

Hello, cat. We haven't met, but I believe I threw away a bag of your vomit once.

Maybe the cat served as a sort of doorman, and his telepathy was better than his digestion, because Brooke Digby came flying through the door, socks-clad, before I ever got a chance to ring the bell.

"Tater!" She flung herself at Percy.

He laughed and spun her around. "Hey, Tot."

When their little reunion was over and Brooke was

on her own feet again, he glanced at me. "It was funny when we were eight. We loved tater tots."

"Cute," I said. I might have pointed out that it grew progressively less cute (and more nauseating) for each year beyond eight, but I hated to ruin their moment. Besides, I was in no position to criticize other people's childhood jargon, given that my sister Sophie and I had formed our own quirks of speech around that same age. "So you guys go way back." *And you never said so when I told you where we were going.*

If that last telepathic message reached Percy, he didn't show it. He was still smiling, mostly at Brooke. "Yeah, we were the same year in school."

Brooke snorted. "That's one way to put it."

So it was like that, then.

Percy ran a hand through his dark hair. "So how long are you in town for?"

"I'm ... not sure." Brooke crossed her arms and looked down at her feet, which I had no doubt were getting mighty cold mighty fast, since her great hurry to see Percy had prevented her from pausing to put on shoes. "Bonnie just got engaged."

"I heard," he said. "Who's the lucky guy?"

"Bo, he's the new chef at Rapunzel's."

"Oh, we all know who Bo is," said Percy.

That we did. Bo Blue had recently won one of the big televised chef competitions. It had been quite a score for Rapunzel's to get him; if we hadn't had a few celebrity chefs of our own at Tybryd, we might have been jealous.

He was also one of those young hotshot types. I couldn't see him marrying a small-town girl—or staying long in the small town. Unless his persona was just an act for the show, which was entirely possible. I'd never met him in person.

"I haven't had his food yet," I said, "but my boss and I have an appointment for a tasting in a couple of weeks. I'm pretty excited to try it."

Tybryd had four restaurants, two cafes, a bakery, and a small winery; we had ample resources for handling our food needs in house. But groups with longer events often wanted to mix things up and go off campus for a night. Rapunzel's was one of our go-to recommendations, which meant the event planners got the fabulous perk of a free dinner whenever Ron Digby hired a new chef.

Brooke gave me the briefest of nods before looking back at Percy. "It was definitely a whirlwind romance kind of thing. They've only known each other a couple months, if you can believe it. But I wanted to be here for her, you know, to do dress shopping and stuff. All the stuff you'd usually do with your mom."

Percy's face sobered. "How is your mom?"

"Not great, actually. Things have gone downhill."

"I'm sorry," he said, and I echoed his words. I was acquainted with Ron Digby only in his professional capacity as the owner of Rapunzel's. I'd never met nor even seen his wife, and I knew nothing about her. But whatever the exact situation was, it seemed clear the woman was ill.

With a shrug, Brooke looked away, toward the front door. "That's why my visit's open-ended. I may just stick around and work from here until …" She shrugged again.

"For a while. To help with her. It's a lot for Dad to handle."

"That's good of you," Percy said. They'd been standing pretty close together; he took a step back and angled his body to better include me in the conversation. "Brooke's a world traveler, usually."

"Oh?" I asked.

Brooke rolled her eyes at him before smiling at me. "It's not as glamorous as he's making it sound. I'm a consultant."

"She's the youngest partner her firm's ever had." There was a definite note of pride in Percy's voice.

Laughing, Brooke poked him in the ribs. "Look who's stalking! Did you come here to spy on me through the windows?"

The question clearly did not apply to me, but I held up my Tybryd-branded shopping bag of samples. "We just stopped on our way by, to drop these off for Bonnie. As promised."

"Oh right, I forgot." Brooke gave me a thoughtful look, as if really noticing me for the first time, before turning back to Percy. "So, you two ...?"

The vigor with which Percy waved off the implication was frankly insulting. "Just friends! And coworkers, obviously. We're on our way to run another errand." He stuffed his hands into his pockets, head bowed. "We're actually going to check on Keith Howell's pets. He was murdered last night."

"Murdered," Brooke repeated, eyes shifting to me. "So that's what happened?" The sadness in her face looked genuine. Unlike the last ex of Percy's I'd met

(Why did Percy have so many exes? And why did I have to meet them?), I thought this one might actually be a nice person.

"I'm afraid so," I said.

"Who was murdered?" Bonnie came out onto the porch, her expression markedly more pleasant than I'd ever seen it before. She greeted Percy with a fierce hug. "Perce! Did you come to congratulate me, or to see if Brooke would agree to a double wedding?"

"Bonnie," Brooke said sharply.

"Oh, or maybe a triple wedding!" Bonnie ignored her sister and grinned at Percy. "I hear Elaine got engaged, too! Tell her congrats for me, will you?"

"Bonnie," Brooke said again. "We were just talking about what happened with Keith Howell. Turns out he was murdered."

"And like I said last night, it's about time. Are those for me?" Without waiting for an answer, Bonnie snatched the bag out of my hand and poked her head inside. "Awesome, thank you. Oh!" She looked from me to Percy and back again, then laughed. "Is that why you brought him?"

I had no idea what this meant. "Is what why?"

"When I said I wanted to talk to your supervisor, I didn't mean you had to go that far."

I faked a laugh. It was the best I could do. "No no, Percy's helping me with something else, after."

"They're going to check on Keith's pets," Brooke provided.

"Nice of you." Bonnie could not have sounded more bored with this information. "Anyway, Brooke convinced me I was being unreasonable yesterday, so. I guess I'll stick with you."

I supposed I was expected to express some gratitude, but what I was actually doing was revising my conclusion that Brooke Digby was a nice person. And maybe cursing her, just a little bit.

"So we were talking," Bonnie went on, "and what if we got married on a Sunday? I looked at that calendar yesterday, and I'm pretty sure you have oodles of Sundays free."

I shook my head. "One wedding per weekend. Tybryd rules, I'm sorry."

"Even if we used the little inn?" Brooke asked. I was impressed with her knowledge of Tybryd. As far as I knew, only the staff called the little inn that. Its official title was Shining Rock Hall, despite there being no rock there, shiny or otherwise. But maybe she'd heard it called the little inn by Percy, in between bites of tater tots.

"Even if," I said. "It's a site-wide policy. We want to make sure every bride feels special on her day."

"And the day *after* her day, I guess?" Bonnie's voice had that tantrum edge. "She needs to feel *that* special, and I don't get to feel special at *all*?"

I braced myself. "Our wedding packages include a weekend stay for the couple, so we block off the whole thing. We book the event spaces for other things besides weddings on Sundays. Conferences and retreats, things like that."

Thankfully, Brooke cut in before Bonnie could work up to a full conniption. Putting her hand on her sister's shoulder, she asked, "What about during the week? Like a Thursday or something? That might be a good compromise."

"What is going on out here?" Ron Digby stalked out onto the porch, looking even more thunderous than his youngest daughter. But he stopped when he saw Percy, and the storm in his puffy, deep-set eyes abated. A little, anyway. "Perce. Nice to see you. Been ages."

Percy shook his hand. "Too long, Ron. Good to see you, as well."

"I'd invite you in, but it's not the best time for it." Ron turned to his daughters (without having so much as glanced at me), and his face clouded over again. "Girls, I told you you need to keep it down today. You've gotten your mother all worked up."

That cowed both Digby sisters. And maybe took twenty years off their ages, because they looked like frightened little girls as they stumbled through their goodbyes and promises to be in touch.

Within seconds, Percy and I were alone on the porch, the front door having been closed softly but unceremoniously in our faces.

"What was that about?" I asked Percy, as soon as we'd walked out of hearing distance.

"Julie Digby has cancer," he said shortly. Apparently considering this a complete explanation, he opened the Jeep's passenger-side door for me.

But sad as that was, I was sure there was more to it. Because the Digbys hadn't seemed sad; they'd seemed *scared*. Whatever had just happened felt a lot more sinister than respect for a sick woman's rest.

Chapter Six

"So," I said as Percy exited the highway. "Brooke Digby."

Possibly sensing that I meant to torture him, he squirmed a little in his seat. "What about her?"

"Well, it doesn't look great, does it?"

He kept his eyes dead straight on the road. "What doesn't?"

"She rolls into town, one of her family's mortal enemies turns up dead. It's very suspicious timing."

Percy laughed and scowled at the same time, which was no mean feat. "Brooke Digby did not kill anybody. She won't even kill a spider."

"I don't know." I sucked my breath through my teeth in an exaggerated impression of regret. "I don't think I can just take your word for it. You don't seem very objective."

He squirmed again. "Minerva, knock it off. Brooke's got it hard enough without you picking on her."

"I'm not picking on her, I'm picking on you." I gave his shoulder a light smack. "I'm only teasing."

"Well then, knock that off too."

I wanted to ask what he meant by how hard Brooke had it, apart from the obvious, and what exactly was going on with her mysterious mother. But the finality in his voice suggested I'd snarked myself right out of the opportunity.

Not that he didn't deserve it, my snark being born of a misgiving that he'd decided to come with me today only because I was stopping by the Digbys—and because he was hoping Brooke would be there. I more than half suspected he didn't really care about Buckingham and Suffolk at all.

We rode in silence for an awkward minute, until Percy started talking about Keith again. It seemed murder was the only safe subject for us today.

"If you're so eager to pin it on a feud, you might want to start with the Towes. Not that I think Gerry Towe runs around killing spiders, either." He rubbed his jaw. "Although come to think of it, Milton Towe probably does. Regardless, legend has it that Molly Towe was the one who put the curse on the Howells. Somewhere in the early 1900s, I think."

"Curse?" I sat up straighter. "What curse?"

"You don't know about the curse?"

"Would I be asking if I did?"

"Okay, so Molly Towe was the local"—Percy raised his fingers off the steering wheel long enough to make finger quotes—"witch, and she had some big dispute with Ian Howell. Some of the stories have it being about land, some say it had to do with an affair. Whatever. The point is, she puts this curse on Ian, and the whole Howell family while she's at it. They'll never have daughters, only sons."

"That's a weird curse," I said. "Wouldn't you do it the other way around, to make sure the family name dies out?"

"Sure, you probably would, if the story were true. But if you're making something up it has to fit reality, right?"

"So the story is made up?"

"No," Percy said solemnly. "Bryd Hollow is actually populated by witches, and the curse is real."

"Okay, smartypants, so the reality is what?"

"Did you just call me smartypants?"

"I did, and I'd do it again."

He snickered. "All right, since you asked so nicely, the reality is that the Howell family runs through Bryd Hollow in an unbroken line, father to son, for ... well, I guess since the early 1900s. Every generation has one or two sons, but not a single daughter."

"So every single person in Bryd Hollow who has Howell blood is actually *named* Howell?" I chewed at my thumbnail, struck by how strange that was. What were the odds of a hundred daughterless years? "I mean, there would be branches on the family tree, anywhere there were multiple sons, but not a single other name. Unless one of them took his wife's name instead of the other way around, but I'm guessing they weren't a particularly forward-thinking family."

"All Howells," Percy agreed. "Only there aren't any branches left either. The home Keith's mother lives in is in Buchanan County, but up until yesterday the only person in Bryd Hollow by that name was Keith." He paused to listen to the tinny voice of the GPS tell him to turn left at the next light. "Unless Alan moves back, which I highly doubt, the Howell line in Bryd Hollow just ended."

"And does Alan have kids?" I asked. And if he did, were they boys? Or did the curse only apply to Howells actually residing in Bryd Hollow?

"No idea," said Percy. "I don't really know him. He used to spend summers here as a kid, but he was a lot older than me, or what seemed like a lot older back then. More like my sister Gwen's age."

Fascinating as the Howell family curse was, I was even more interested in the mention of the estranged Baird daughter. It was the first time I'd heard any Baird speak Gwen's name. Frankly, I would have liked to use the opening to do a little prying, but by then Percy had pulled into the parking lot at the county animal shelter.

The young woman behind the counter was friendly, but baffled by our request for visitation. After clarifying several times that all we wanted to do was *see* Suffolk and Buckingham, and not actually *take* them (which seemed to disappoint her greatly), she led us back to the cat room. They behaved much better together than apart, she explained, so Buckingham had been allowed to share a cage with his feline friend.

Both cat and bird eyed me morosely as I approached. "Hey guys," I cooed in my most soothing pet-mom tone. "We just wanted to see how you are. Are you doing okay in there?"

While Suffolk hissed and threw himself against the

back of the cage, Buckingham squawked loudly enough to wake his recently deceased master, jumped forward, and tried his best to bite my nose.

"Odsbodikins!" I stepped back and put my hands on my hips. "Really, Buckingham? Again?"

Buckingham replied with a chorus of shrieks. Suffolk lost no time backing up his friend, howling at me and batting at the bars with his paws, claws extended.

I tried the soothing voice again. "All right. Easy." Unmoved, Buckingham and Suffolk continued to show their displeasure. A few of the other cats began joining in with meows and calls of their own. "I understand you guys are scared. I just—"

"What are you doing?" someone called from the doorway. "Get away from them!"

I turned to find a gentleman I assumed was one of the shelter people, come to reprimand us for the disturbance we were causing (well, I was causing). But as he came closer, I realized this must be Alan Howell. Short, slim, and hook-nosed, he'd have been the spitting image of his father if his lank hair had been gray rather than brown.

Hadn't Percy said Alan lived on the west coast? He must have dropped everything and gotten straight on a plane, to have gotten across the country so soon after Keith's death. Which might have explained why he was dressed so inappropriately for the weather, in shorts that were frayed at the hems, a faded t-shirt *(I'm Not Anti-Social—I Just Don't Like You)*, and filthy sneakers that had clearly seen better days. Maybe he'd been gardening when he got the call.

"Alan!" Percy stepped forward and held out a hand, which Alan ignored. "We were so sorry to hear about Keith. We had no idea you'd get here so quickly."

"So you decided to come and try to steal my father's pets before I got here?"

"What?" Percy dropped his hand. "No, of course not."

Who would want them? I added silently, then immediately reprimanded myself for being so uncharitable. Toward Suffolk and Buckingham, that is. I had no quibbles with my instant dislike of Alan Howell. He was looking at Percy like he'd just caught us beating the animals, as opposed to the other way around.

"We were checking on them," I said. "Making sure they're okay, until you or somebody else could take them home."

"Well, I'm taking them now, so you can go." Alan pursed his lips as he looked me up and down. Clearly he found my explanation suspicious. "And you're who, now?"

"Minerva Biggs. Nice to meet you, I'm so sorry it's under such awful circumst—"

"Briggs?"

"Biggs."

"Minnie Biggs?" Alan let out a harsh bark of laughter.

I gave Percy a pointed look. I hoped this thoroughly demonstrated what poor company making that joke put him in. Percy, for his part, avoided my eye while he clearly struggled not to laugh.

"Well," I said to Alan, "I'm very sorry for your loss. Keith was …"

I swallowed. I could hardly say he was loved, could I? Or that he was a good man. Or that he'd be missed. "… too young." That would have to do. I'd have put Keith in his sixties, which would qualify as a life cut short.

Alan snorted. "Yeah, I'm sorry for my loss, too." He shifted his belligerent look to Percy. "So? What are you still hanging around for? Buckingham doesn't talk, you know, if you were hoping he'd call out the name of my dad's killer and solve your case for you."

"Solve my case …" Percy tossed his hands. "What? I'm not investigating your father's death, Alan."

"No? You sure act like Bryd Hollow and everyone in it is your personal property. Most of the time, anyway. But I guess when it comes to actually being useful …" Alan scoffed. "That's when you finally decide to know your place, huh?"

Percy's jaw tightened, but he didn't rise to the bait. "Like Minerva said, we came to check on Suffolk and Buckingham."

"Well, I told you, I'm taking them. So there's nothing to check." Alan made a shooing motion with both hands. "Run along, now. Get."

Get? One thing was for sure: Alan Howell was every bit as charming as his father.

∾

A MESSAGE from Percy popped up on my computer screen at six-thirty that same night. *Working late?*

Yeah—why? I replied. *Checking that I'm making up for the totally wasted trip to see the cat and bird?*

Checking whether you and Plant want to take a break for a walk. I'll probably be here half the night. Thanks to the totally wasted trip to see the cat and bird.

"Well, whose fault is that?" I muttered. "You were the one who was so desperate for the chance to run into Brooke Digby." But all I typed back was, *Sure. Where and when?*

Maze entrance, 15?

I smiled. Percy always suggested the hedge maze; apparently he'd been in love with it since he was a little boy. I wasn't even sure if dogs were technically allowed in there, but I supposed when you had a Baird with you, there were no rules. Besides, nobody else was going to be using it on a cold and cloudy February night. *We'll be there.*

I spent the first five of those fifteen minutes trying to motivate Plant, who at the ripe old age of three (and a half) appeared to be entering his lazy years, and did not appreciate evening walks. In the end I was obliged to use the word *Percy* not once but twice, and even then there was an audible groan when he got up.

Fat snowflakes were floating languidly down when we got outside, which made me smile, but knocked Plant's enthusiasm level down another notch. He trudged along, head bowed, certain he was the most abused dog in the big wide world.

Until we got close enough to the maze entrance for him to see Percy, at which point Plant rushed forward with his signature full-body wiggle-wag, weather and walk and even me forgotten. He immediately snatched off one of Percy's gloves, but the leash hindered his ability to prance.

"Leave it," I said, reaching for it at the same time. Plant relinquished it, though not without reluctance.

"Sorry buddy, I'm always getting you in trouble, aren't I?" Percy squatted down to give Plant some scritches and accept a bit of slobber in return. "Are you going to be okay in the snow?" he asked me. "I didn't really think about women's shoes when I made the suggestion."

"*I'm* fine." I handed him back his glove. "This snow won't stick. Plant, on the other hand, is feeling a little mopey about it."

Percy stood and looked down at Plant, who was still wagging. "Doesn't look mopey to me."

"His heart's been warmed by his love for you, but that spark will fade."

Percy pressed a hand to his chest. "How dare you suggest."

As usual, I was lost within seconds of entering the maze. The paths were lit by ground lights (which showed off the snow to lovely effect), but darkness wasn't my issue so much as my terrible sense of direction. I never went in there unless it was with Percy. He'd been doing it so long he took the proper turns with neither hesitation nor any apparent thought.

"So," I said, "Alan Howell seems nice."

Percy laughed. "Yeah, he's quite a guy."

"I thought you said you didn't know him."

"I don't, really."

"He seemed to know you."

"Are you implying that his description of me was accurate?"

I pretended to consider this. "You *are* kind of bossy."

"I guess, but I think this was more a case of Alan painting all Bairds with the Clifford Baird brush." Percy glanced at me, smiling a little. "Suffolk and Buckingham seemed nice, too. Do you think they were born that way, or trained to it? Or maybe they're just grumpy about having such stupid names."

"I worked at Noah's Bark for a while. I have definitely heard stupider names. Although ..." I frowned, remembering something from the day before. (Had it really only been the day before, that Keith Howell had been alive?) "Why do they have those names? I asked Keith if he had a thing about English dukedoms, and he actually said he did. But then we got interrupted before he could get into it."

"You know." Percy fluttered one hand. "The royalty thing."

"I don't know. What royalty thing?"

"Oh yeah, I guess you wouldn't know. You didn't really know any of them." He gestured to the left, waiting for Plant and me, who were on that side, to turn the corner first before following. "They liked to claim kinship to the Tudors."

I looked back over my shoulder. "The *Tudors*?"

"Yep."

"The Tudors." I stopped walking and turned to face Percy. "Of Britain."

He laughed. "Don't get too excited."

"I'm not getting excited." I was definitely getting excited.

"Good, because my family never put much stock in it. And you know if there were anything to it, Alistair Baird would've been all over it."

"Why would your family be thinking about the Howells' ancestry either way?"

"The Bairds and the Howells are related. You didn't know that, either?"

I faked a guilty look. "You caught me. I haven't committed all the Bryd Hollow family trees to memory yet."

"Okay, smartypants."

"What a ridiculous word."

Percy smirked and nodded ahead. "Keep walking, we're almost to the center. So the first Howell in Bryd Hollow was a distant relative of Alistair Baird's mother, some fourteenth cousin fifteen times removed, or whatever."

I laughed. "That would be distant."

"I don't think they much liked being the poor relation, hired as an act of charity. They've always resented us." Percy rubbed the back of his neck. "Although that could just be because my father and his father and his father were jerks."

"And his father," I added.

"The point is, they've never made a big deal about the connection."

"Yet they make a big deal about this connection to English royalty?"

Percy shrugged. "I can't speak for Alan, but Keith sure seemed proud of it. His parents too, I think."

One final turn brought us to the center of the maze. Percy brushed away a few flakes of snow that clung to one of the stone benches, and we sat while Plant busied himself with trying to catch the falling snow in his mouth.

I wrapped Plant's leash around my wrist and drummed my fingers against my leg, thinking about the Howells and the Tudors and not at all about how good Percy smelled. "It wasn't exactly *English* royalty, though. Not at first."

"What do you mean?" he asked.

"Alistair's mother was Welsh." I pointed at him. "You guys are part Welsh."

"It's a small part now, but yeah."

I might not have known every family tree in Bryd Hollow, but I'd at least filled the gaps in my Tybryd knowledge before coming to work for the Bairds. *Baird* was Scottish, as were Alistair's father's forebears. But the words *Tybryd* and *Bryd Hollow* came from Alistair's Welsh half, on his mother's side.

And that was the full extent of my—or anybody's—understanding. If Alistair had ever told how he'd arrived at the name of his grand estate, the story hadn't survived. *Ty* was a Welsh word for *house*, so that part was easy enough. But *bryd* could have meant a few things: *when, time, intent, aim*. None of which were especially good names for towns or houses.

I'd formed my own possibly ridiculous theory, based on my extensive internet-search-expertise in the Welsh language, that the *bryd* part came from *ysbryd*, which meant *spirit* or *ghost*. Ghost Hollow. House of Ghosts. Now those were names I could get behind. All hollows should be haunted, in my view.

The question was, exactly who was haunting this one? "And the Howells were related to Alistair's mother," I said. "Isn't Howell a Welsh name?"

"I have no idea," said Percy.

"Because Henry Tudor, the guy who became Henry VII, he was Welsh. *And* the Duke of Suffolk was Henry VIII's best friend."

Percy's mouth quirked. "So you're taking a few guys being Welsh as proof of a claim that was probably made up by some drunk Howell three hundred years ago?"

"Of course not."

"Because there've been a lot of Welsh people."

"I know that. I'm just saying it's *possible*, even if it's highly unlikely, that there's some distant tie between the Howells and the Tudors." I clapped his shoulder. "It's up to us to figure out whether it's really there or not."

"And we need to figure this out why?"

Of course. Not being a history dork, Percy had no idea why my heart had started pounding just a little harder. (Okay, maybe it had *started* pounding a little harder when he sat down so close to me that our knees were touching, but that was not the point. The point was, it was pounding now for purely scholarly reasons.) "Well I guess *we* don't, but *I* do. The knife."

"What about it?"

"I have a vague memory of notation knives being Italian, but that might just be because I associate Renaissance stuff with Italy. Or maybe they were French. And of course neither of those is English, is it?"

"Um ... no ..." Percy said. "Is this a trick question?"

I chewed at my lip. "And the English Renaissance isn't even the same as the Italian Renaissance. So I guess that's a lot stacked against this being related. But still."

Noting that Percy's eyes were glazing over, I waved all this away. "The point is, notation knives were *sixteenth century* things."

"And?"

His interest sounded more polite than genuine, but that was all right. I had more than enough blossoming enthusiasm for the both of us. "And there was one Tudor or another on the throne of England for that *entire century*."

Percy burst out laughing.

I crossed my arms. "What?"

"You're just *really excited* about Keith Howell getting stabbed with this special knife."

"I know, I'm awful." I ducked my head, embarrassed. "It's just, I taught American history, but British history is my *thing*. I named my dog *Plantagenet,* for pete's sake. I wrote my thesis on Richard III."

"And was he a Tudor?"

"Of course not, he was a Plantagenet. The last Plantag—are you teasing me?"

"I would never."

I tossed my head. "Well, his niece did marry Henry Tudor."

Having heard his name used so many times in such short succession, Plant came to rest his head on my knee, wagging his tail. I scratched his head. "It's just been a while since any of this knowledge was useful."

"And you think it might be useful now?" Percy nodded and answered himself before I got a chance to. "Ruby obviously thought so, or she wouldn't have called you last night."

"Yeah, well, I doubt she'll continue to think so. In my experience, Ruby is not a fan of connecting present-day crimes to the past."

I, on the other hand, was. And there were a lot of connections to the past in Keith Howell's murder. Feuds dating back centuries. Ancient (okay, maybe more *kind of old* than *ancient*, but still) family curses. A notation knife, of all things.

Even—maybe, vaguely—*Tudors*.

And those were just the ones I knew about.

There were just too many historical ties here for me to resist. And I really wanted to know what the story was with that knife. If you want the truth, I kind of *needed* to know.

"Well." I gave Plant's ear a final scratch and stood, my mind made up. "It's not going to be fun, but I am definitely going to have to pay Alan Howell a visit. Saturday, maybe. I'll bring him a pot pie."

"A pot pie." Percy blinked at me as he got to his feet. "Because ... Tudors ... ate pot pies?"

"Because that's what you do, when somebody dies, you bring their family a chicken pot pie. Casserole is acceptable in a pinch, but pie is always better. Only amateurs bring lasagna."

"Obviously."

"Exactly. Honestly, how do you not know this? What kind of neighbor are you?"

He gave me a sheepish half-smile, one dimple only. "The kind who doesn't bake his own pies."

"Well, here's your chance to learn how to pay proper condolences." I raised a brow at him in challenge. Mostly because I was kind of scared to face Alan Howell by myself. "If you're brave enough to come along?"

Chapter Seven

"WE'RE NOT GOING to bring him?"

It was hard to say who looked more disappointed: Percy, who'd asked the question, or Plant, who seemed to sense he was the *him* not being brought. Plant heaved a long-suffering sigh and flopped down on the rug in front of the refrigerator. Percy, who'd previously picked us up for hikes but never been properly inside my apartment, shook his head at me and resumed nosing around my kitchen.

"The whole point is to try to get Alan to invite us in," I said. "You know, like a polite person would do. Which I'll agree is a stretch goal, but I doubt Plant would improve our chances. I don't think Suffolk and Buckingham would think very highly of him."

"Probably not." Percy opened my pantry door, pulled out a pouch of chili-flavored quinoa, and scrunched up his face. "This is the kind of thing you eat?"

"Excuse me." I crossed my arms. "We don't all live in mansions that come equipped with professional chefs."

He looked at me over his shoulder, open-mouthed. "Yours came equipped with an *amateur* chef? How can you live like that?"

"Ha very ha. You're so funny, Percy, that's why the ladies love you."

"That's not why." He paused a beat as he replaced the quinoa, no doubt to see if I would rise to that bait. Which I did not. The more time we spent together, the more flirting with Percy felt like a dangerous business.

I don't want his life, I reminded myself. It was becoming something of a mantra. *Not that I've been offered it.*

"At least you have taffy." He picked up a large box of saltwater taffy (one of three on that shelf) and chose a piece.

"I always have taffy."

"One of my favorite things about you. Anyway, you're in luck. I'm supposed to tell you you're invited to my mansion next Sunday after church, for a meal prepared by our professional chef. Not tomorrow, the Sunday after."

"You're supposed to tell me? Who extended this invitation?" I didn't love the sound of this. Probably because it sounded like he'd made his mother invite me over, possibly against her will.

"All of us, I guess. My mom is having the brunch, as an engagement thing, but Elaine was going to call and invite you. Except I told her I was seeing you today, so she told me to tell you. She figures while she's got Phil there too, you guys might have a chance to talk about the wedding."

"Oh!" That sounded harmless enough. "Okay."

"And then my mother chimed in all excited about how *adorable* you are, and how *wonderful* it would be if you came, since she hasn't seen you in *ages*. You know how she gets."

"No mention of the fact that the reason she hasn't seen me in ages is because she fired me?"

"Bygones." Percy closed the pantry door and turned to lean against it, arms crossed. "So you'll come?"

"Sure."

"Great." He nodded at the chicken pie on my counter. "Think it's cool enough yet?"

I brushed my fingers over the crust and found it warm, but not hot, to the touch. "It's not ideal, but it's close enough for the likes of Alan Howell." I took it off the cooling rack and popped it into the waiting pie carrier, then sighed as I clasped the lid. "He's never going to return this container, is he?"

"Probably not." Percy picked it up. "A small price to pay for an audience with a Tudor king though, no?"

"I guess, but I really like that one."

"I'll buy you a new one." He held the pie carrier up to eye level and squinted inside. "You used real stuff in this, right? The crust isn't made out of quinoa or something?"

"I will have you know I'm a good cook. Plant, come and get your bone."

"Maybe we should just stay and eat it, then."

I didn't bother to answer, just gave Percy a little shove

toward the door. I wasn't looking forward to this mission either, but if I wanted to find out more about the knife, it had to be done.

Keith's house—Alan's house, now—was a short drive, and I could still feel a little warmth through the bottom of the pie carrier as I brought it up the walk. Alan was on the front porch with the man I'd seen talking to Roark the night Keith was murdered. Ollie Gilroy, as I'd been told. On this occasion, neither man was talking so much as yelling.

"For the last time, I don't have it!" Alan roared. "What in sam-heck would I want with a daggum *ferret hammock*?"

"Your no-good thief of a father probably passed it off as something he made himself. Probably sold it already." Ollie jabbed a pudgy finger at Alan. "I'll check with Gretchen, see if I don't!"

Alan scowled at us as we climbed the porch steps, then scowled even harder at Ollie. "You do that, Gilroy. I've got guests, as you can see."

Being the lesser of two evils had its perks. Without a word of greeting, Alan held his front door open and ushered us inside, before slamming it in Ollie Gilroy's face.

There were no immediate attacks, but I did hear a fair amount of squawking from above. I looked up the stairs to find a baby gate at the top, behind which Suffolk sat glaring, tail twitching slowly. I supposed Buckingham was in a cage somewhere. That must have been a rude awakening for him.

I held the pie out to Alan, who made no move to take it.

"What do you two want?" he asked.

"Alan, really!" A woman with a heavily highlighted bob who I was pretty sure was pregnant (but not far enough along that you'd say so, in case you were wrong) hurried through the living room from the direction of the kitchen, wiping her hands on a towel. "Hello, I'm Tracey Howell."

For a second I could only stare at her. She looked so *normal* to be married to Alan Howell. I guessed I'd just figured he would be divorced by now, if he'd ever been married at all.

Percy jumped into the silence and introduced us both. Remembering my manners at last, I handed Tracey the pie. "We just wanted to pay our respects, and give you this chicken pie."

"Oh! Oh, how kind. Not many people have ..." She looked a little flustered, then gave me a bright smile and stepped aside, gesturing toward the living room. "Come in. I'm so sorry for the noise. That bird never seems to stop."

"I'm sorry if we've come at a bad time," I offered.

"No, no." Tracey waved this away with a flap of her kitchen towel. "I mean, they're all bad times, aren't they? Alan got the call, we got on a plane just as soon as we could drop the kids off at my mother's, and it's been chaos ever since." She patted the side of the pie container. "This will help a lot. Alan does most of the cooking, and he's been so preoccupied. So thank you. Won't you—"

She turned toward the living room again, then

stopped herself with a grimace. Maybe the plaid was too much for her, too. "Why don't we go into the kitchen for some coffee? I can reliably make coffee."

Alan made no move to follow us; instead he pulled out his phone and stalked up the stairs as he jabbed at the screen. Apart from asking why we were there, he hadn't said a thing to us.

A few minutes later, Percy and I were settled at the table with mugs of decaf instant coffee that I gave my best impression of sipping from time to time. Tracey rounded it out with a plate of Oreos, which I was much more kindly disposed toward.

"You mentioned dropping the kids off," Percy said. "How many do you have?"

"Two. Twin boys. And another on the way, as I'm sure you noticed." With a proud smile, Tracey pulled out her phone and showed off a few pictures of two boys in various sports uniforms. They looked maybe five or six, and resembled her much more than their father, a nice bit of good luck for them.

Percy gave my knee a light smack under the table, as if I'd otherwise have failed to notice that the curse of sons remained unbroken.

"You have a lovely family," I said. *And a cursed one, apparently*.

"We didn't want to bring them," Tracey said, "given the circumstances of Keith's death. I thought about staying home too, actually, but Alan ..." She cleared her throat. "He doesn't want to deal with a funeral home, so. He needs a lot of help with the funeral."

"He ... isn't using a funeral home?" Percy looked aghast.

"You don't need one, for the most part," Tracey said. "Home funerals are allowed in North Carolina. A fun fact I learned just yesterday."

"But then ..." Percy didn't seem to know how to finish his sentence.

Tracey took pity on him. "Obviously we can't *embalm* Keith ourselves, if that's what you're asking. We'll be outsourcing that part. But the rest, yes, you can handle yourself. We'll do the service graveside, and the rest here. There won't be a viewing, so we won't need to prepare the body the way a mortician would."

"Still," I said, "making so many arrangements in such a short amount of time, it must be overwhelming. Especially when you're grieving. If it's not too forward to say so, I'm an event planner. I'd be more than happy to help you. You know, just ... informally."

Funerals were a lot like weddings, when it came down to it: flowers, catering, decisions about seating and booze. I was sure there must be something I could do for Tracey. I felt awful for her. She looked exhausted already.

Then again, maybe that was how she always looked. It had to be exhausting just to be married to Alan Howell.

"That is so nice of you," she said. "You're right about it being overwhelming. But I mean, we don't have ..." She paused, turning her mug in her hands. "The flights were like a thousand apiece—"

"I wouldn't dream of charging you," I interrupted. I felt almost as awkward as she seemed to. I'd hoped she would interpret the word *informally* as *free*; I hadn't been able to think of another way to say it without sounding insulting about it.

Tracey exhaled heavily. I had the impression it was relief. "I wouldn't ask for charity, but I really have no idea how to do this, and Alan's so busy settling estate stuff."

"It's not charity," I said. "This is a small town. Neighbors helping neighbors, and all that."

Percy picked up Tracey's phone from the table and started tapping the screen. "I'm putting both Minerva's number and mine in your contacts." He flashed those dimples of his. "I am not an event planner, and nowhere near as useful as she is, in general. But if I can help with anything, please don't hesitate to call."

Tracey's return smile was downright radiant. I felt pretty relieved myself; we might be intruding on a grieving family for the secret purpose of fishing for information, but at least we'd done some good.

"So." Much more relaxed now, Tracey bit into a cookie and leaned back in her chair, hand on her belly. "Did you two know Keith well?"

"All my life," Percy said smoothly. "He was a vital part of Bryd Hollow." Smooth, but maybe not smooth enough. Tracey gave him a look that suggested she knew he was choosing his adjectives with diplomacy.

Seeing an opening to bring the conversation around to the Howell family tree, I added, "The Howells are such a distinguished family here. One of the founding families, as I understand it. Practically royalty." *Now who's the smooth one?*

Percy shot me an amused look, but if Tracey associated the word *royalty* with her husband's family, she didn't show it. She gave me a slightly befuddled nod and said, "Well, if you knew him, do you have any ideas about what might have happened to him? That police chief hasn't been able to tell us much, in the way of suspects. I don't think she has any leads at all."

"Ruby will get to the bottom of it," Percy assured her.

"Let's hope so," Tracey said. "Personally, I'm already halfway to accusing Ollie Gilroy."

"I don't know Ollie well," I said. *Or at all.* "He looked upset, when we saw him on the porch just now."

Tracey snorted. "*Upset* is putting it mildly. He's been over here constantly with one complaint and demand after another."

"What kind of demands?" Percy asked.

"That we return stolen property, mostly."

I sat up straighter. Property like priceless knives?

But Tracey went on, "He swears Keith was in the habit of stealing packages off his porch."

So, no. Property like ferret hammocks, a phrase I belatedly remembered hearing outside. "It's just such an unusual crime," I said, then added with what I hoped was delicacy, "The choice of weapon, I mean."

Tracey took another cookie and pulled it apart. "That was just a weapon of opportunity, though. As in, it must have been nearby when whatever argument they were having got out of hand. No one would *plan* to come into Keith's house and kill him with his own knife. You'd bring your own knife, don't you think, if it was premeditated?"

I tried not to look too eager. "The knife was Keith's?"

"Oh, yes. Alan tells me it was a family heirloom."

"*Is* a family heirloom." Alan stamped into the kitchen. "It's still my property, whatever Ruby Walker might think she has to say about it."

Percy turned in his chair to face Alan. "Ruby's denying it's yours?"

"What difference does it make whether she acknowledges it's mine, if she won't *give* it to me?" Alan pitched his voice high in apparent imitation of Ruby, although Ruby's voice was not particularly high. I guessed it was just his generic female voice. "It's evidence, Mr. Howell. I cannot turn it over to you at this time."

"But I'm sure she really can't, during an active investigation," I said—stating what I assumed was obvious to everybody in the room, Alan included. "I'm sure she'll return it to you eventually."

"*Eventually* don't pay the rent." Alan scowled at me. "Besides being a family heirloom, it's also family business. By which I mean, it isn't *your* business. We've got a lot to do, so if there's nothing else?"

"Alan." Blushing, Tracey gave Percy and me a rueful look. "Please excuse his manners. Like I said, things have been a little crazy."

"Of course," Percy said.

"Not at all," I said at the same time. We stood in unison. Tracey followed suit.

Alan went right on standing in the doorway, looking cranky. "Don't need anyone making excuses for me."

"It was so nice to meet you both," Tracey said, overly loud. "I hope to see you on Thursday, at the funeral?"

She looked nervous as she asked the question, like maybe she was afraid nobody would show up to mourn Keith. I could've told her that was an unfounded concern. Nobody had liked him, sure, but his funeral was still a chance to poke their noses into his business.

Including for me. "Of course," I said. "And I hope you'll be in touch before that, to take me up on my offer."

"What offer?" Alan gave me a suspicious look.

"I'm an event planner over at Tybryd. I thought I might be able to take some of the funeral details off your hands."

Looking highly offended, Alan shifted his gaze to Percy. "We're not having my father's funeral at *Tybryd*."

"No, of course not," Percy agreed.

Heaven forbid. "The event planner part was the main thing," I said.

Alan grunted something unintelligible before saying, "We don't need a Baird's help to bury a Howell. Let's go, I'll show you out."

He did, all the way to the door (where we were met with a fresh chorus of squawks from upstairs), then stood on the porch and watched us drive away. Maybe he was afraid we would steal something, if left to our own devices.

Percy punched the gas pedal maybe a little harder than necessary, like he was in a hurry to leave the Howell house behind.

"You did pretty well, for a bad neighbor," I said.

"I've got natural charm. Didn't do us much good, though. Nothing about your Tudors."

"That was always a long shot, I guess. It's not the kind of thing you talk to strangers about a few days after your father-in-law's murder. But we did find out that the knife was Keith's, not the killer's."

Without taking his eyes off the road, Percy pointed sideways at me. "And if they're calling it an heirloom, either it's real, or they think it is."

I nodded, turning to the window to watch Bryd Hollow whizzing by. "It can't be," I muttered, more to myself than to Percy. We were an ocean and an age away from Renaissance Europe.

But Percy had a point: whether or not it was real, Keith must have thought it was. Which had to mean something, surely, in the context of him having been stabbed in the eye with it.

I looked back at Percy. "*And* we found out Alan wants that knife back pretty badly. And given his little bit of snark about paying the rent, I guess we know why."

"You think he wants to sell it?"

"I think Alan Howell has some money problems. Doing the funeral yourself? There is no reason to torture yourself like that other than to save money. And you saw how Tracey got, when she was afraid I was trying to sell her my services."

"I'm sure you're right, but it's not really relevant to the murder, is it?" Percy, as usual, tapped out a beat on the steering wheel. "Other than to Buckingham and Suffolk. I guess maybe they won't be kept in the style to which they've become accustomed."

"I don't know." I chewed at my lip. "If you need money, and let's say you have a not-great relationship with your father, and your father happens to own something worth, oh I don't know, *millions* of dollars ... that might be tempting, no?"

Percy glanced at me. His chuckle sounded confused. "But he was on the other coast when Keith died."

"So he says."

"So his wife says. Tracey specifically said they got on a plane *after* they got the call about Keith."

I shrugged. "Wives lie for their husbands all the time."

"I guess, but I think I'm okay at reading people, and I didn't get any sense she was lying."

"Me neither. But then, I'm terrible at reading people. And neither of us knows her at all."

Percy raised one hand off the wheel, thumb and forefinger an inch apart. "Small wrinkle in this theory. If Alan wanted to sell the knife to some black-market art dealer or whatever, why would he leave it in his father's eye?"

"I'll admit that's a good question. I asked Ruby the same thing, about whoever the killer was." I drummed my fingers against my leg. "But it could be something simple. Like they were fighting over it and things got out of hand. And then Alan panicked and ran when he saw what he'd done. Keith's front door was open."

Percy reached over to pat my hand. "I hate to be unsupportive, Poirot, but that all sounds pretty unlikely."

"Yeah, maybe."

But also maybe not.

How *had* Alan gotten across the country so quickly?

Chapter Eight

KEITH HOWELL's funeral fell on a day as dismal as the man himself: cold, blustery, and sunless. Rain that occasionally decided it would rather be sleet came steadily down, making little puddles of half slush on the sidewalks around St. Asaph's.

I'd ended up having a fairly large hand in planning the whole affair, and had been surprised, given my conjecture about the state of the Howells' finances, to find their budget fairly reasonable. It seemed to be a point of pride with Alan, that the Howell family dignity not be besmirched by second-rate refreshments or flowers.

Sadly, none of my interactions with him or Tracey had resulted in confessions of either murder or Tudor lineage.

The service was held in the graveyard adjacent to the church, where only Bryd Hollow's most longstanding families had plots. Nobody wanted to stand outside for very long, least of all to honor a man they had nothing nice to say about. It made me a little sad, watching them all fidget beneath their umbrellas, clearly just waiting for it to be over. He'd been an unpleasant guy—to some more than others, apparently—but it was awful to see his passing go not only unmourned but almost unmarked, a chore everybody wanted to cross off their list so they could get to the food and gossip after.

Said food and gossip were offered at the Howell home directly following the service. Despite his insistence on a befitting level of hospitality, Alan walked around looking sour and suspicious, as if concerned somebody might steal something.

Which, to be fair, may have been spot on. Shortly after we arrived, there was a shrieking commotion from above.

We'd shut Suffolk and Buckingham away in the back-most bedroom with a heavy towel over Buckingham's cage, but clearly they'd been disturbed. As Alan was busy admonishing Ruby for her failure to return his heirloom, Tracey gratefully accepted my offer to go investigate.

It turned out the Gilroys had gone upstairs, possibly in search of ferret hammocks, and opened the wrong door. By the time I shooed them out of the room and down the hall, Alan had made it to the staircase.

He stood a couple steps down from the top, quaking with rage. "Looking for something, Gilroy?"

"Yes." Ollie raised his chin. "The bathroom. Margie had something in her eye."

"There's a powder room downstairs," I offered. "If you'll just—"

Alan finished the sentence for me. "Leave. If you'll

just leave. You know perfectly well where the bathrooms are in this house. You were snooping."

"I haven't been in this house in years," Ollie protested. "I can't be expected to rem—"

"Don't care," Alan cut in. "I don't want you here. My father wouldn't have wanted you here."

Marge Gilroy looked to me, presumably for aid, but I only shrugged. I was sure Alan was right that Keith wouldn't have wanted them there. And even I considered disturbing Buckingham (who was still making a headache-inducing amount of noise) an unforgivable offense.

Alan gestured for the indignant Gilroys to precede him down the stairs, then looked back at me. "What do you think you're doing?"

Assuming he was referring to my failure to follow him, I pointed my thumb over my shoulder. "I was just going to try to quiet Buckingham down while you show them out."

He considered this, eyes narrowed, then finally gave me a gruff nod. I was a little surprised; neither Howell had left me alone anywhere in the house before. But Alan was probably just as loathe to deal with the cat and the cockatiel as I was. I gathered that neither had warmed up to his new parents.

I sidled into the spare room, but my attempt at stealth did me no good. Suffolk immediately attacked my ankle. Thankfully I was wearing boots, and he didn't break any skin this time. "Listen, mister, I would never kick an animal, but I will shake you off my leg if I have to."

Something in my tone must've said I meant business, because with a parting hiss, Suffolk stalked to the other side of the room to glower at me from the darkest corner.

I put my hands on my hips. "I get that you're upset. And I'm very sorry for your loss. But you can't just go assaulting people all the time. Tracey will rehome you if you hurt her kids, and who do you think would take you?"

Indifferent to my lecture, Suffolk turned his back on me before lying down. At least Buckingham had quieted somewhat as he watched us, although he started carrying on again when I approached his cage. I replaced the towel, which had been either removed by one of the Gilroys, or displaced by the tumult of Buckingham's displeasure.

Once in the dark, the cockatiel let out a few more squawks, then sank into what I was sure was a very sullen silence. The tension in my head eased tenfold.

My work done, I opened the door exactly as wide as I needed to and not an inch more, lest Suffolk try to escape, and slid out into the hallway.

The question was, where to from there?

Downstairs to help, of course, was the obvious answer. But when was I going to get another chance to be alone upstairs in the Howell house?

What if there was something up here? Some people framed decorative family trees or coats of arms and put them on display. Some had cabinets for their antiques, too, and who knew what other treasures had been kept with the knife?

And some, in my experience, kept old journals on

bookshelves, with no notion of how valuable they were, or what answers might be in them.

I hesitated in the dim hallway, well aware that none of this was justification for snooping. If I was going to do it, I ought to at least acknowledge that it was a ratbag thing to do. And to consider whom I was doing it to; even if I didn't think much of Alan, I liked Tracey pretty well.

On the other hand, what real harm could it do?

I bit my lip, eyes roving from one closed door to another. I'd been up here just yesterday (supervised, of course), mostly to designate a safe space for the pets to spend the reception, and I remembered the layout. Keith had been killed in the bedroom he used as an office. It must have ceased to be an active crime scene some time ago, if Ruby was letting the Howells stay in the house, but I knew the door was locked. The spare bedroom had the pets in it. That left the bathrooms, the master bedroom, and Keith's workshop, used for his pet tailoring and other projects.

I resolved my dilemma by meeting myself halfway: I'd have a quick peek into the workshop, but I wouldn't go into the master bedroom, where Alan and Tracey had presumably taken up residence.

So at most, I would be half a ratbag.

There was a good reason Keith had a workshop separate from his office; the bedrooms were small, and this one was stuffed with trunks, cases, boxes, cabinets, a sewing table, and what looked like a general work table. It was all in disarray. Probably Ruby or Roark or somebody had gone through the room for fingerprints and such. Or maybe Keith had just been a slob.

I flicked the light switch to get a better look at the chaos. There was nothing on the walls, framed or otherwise. No boxes labeled *Evidence Of Tudor Ancestry* or *Priceless Relics*.

An apothecary cabinet stood opposite the door, its multitude of small drawers irresistible. I opened a few of them, glancing through the contents: colored pencils, beads, some jewelry-making supplies (I hadn't realized that had been one of Keith's many businesses), sewing supplies.

One held only a few swatches of fabric in bright colors, turquoise and pink and buttery yellow. I cocked my head at the yellow one, which was on top.

Then frowned. Then pulled out my phone to get a better look with the flashlight. Was that ...

"There you are." Tracey's voice, behind me. "What are you doing in here?"

I managed, only just, not to jump and yelp. I closed the drawer and turned around, putting on a harried face. "Did you hear the Gilroys were up here snooping around?"

"I think everyone heard." She rolled her eyes. "From Buckingham."

"Well, they were in here." This may or may not have been true. They'd been in the room with the pets when I caught them. But they *might* have been in here before that. "And as you can see, it looks like some things have been disturbed."

Tracey glanced around, then shook her head. "I don't

think it's any more disturbed than it was when we got here. Alan said it was always a mess in here."

"Oh. Oh, good. I just wanted to make sure they hadn't gotten into anything. You know, just protecting your ferret hammocks." I said this last with a snicker, and Tracey laughed at the joke.

But she also stepped aside, hand on the doorknob, clearly expecting me to precede her out of the room. And she didn't leave me alone again, not until we were all the way downstairs.

Not that I could blame her. She'd caught me snooping, and I was pretty sure we both knew it. It might have been horribly embarrassing, had I not been distracted from the awkwardness by what I'd seen on that bit of yellow fabric: a tiny black hair. I didn't know whether it belonged to a dog or a cat, but I was sure it didn't belong to a human. I knew animal hair when I saw it.

The presence of animal hair was not, of course, surprising in a house with a cat in it. Suffolk's hair was all over everything. Which probably explained why the police hadn't paid much attention to it, if they'd seen it at all. The workshop wasn't the scene of the crime. Maybe they hadn't even done a thorough forensicwhatsit in there.

The thing was, though, Suffolk was gray. And this hair was black. Maybe the difference was subtle, in some light—but there *was* a difference.

Which meant ... absolutely nothing. Everybody with a pet knew they were constantly distributing that pet's hair everywhere they went, off their sleeves, their coats and sweaters, gloves. I'd surely deposited a few of Plant's black hairs around this house myself. Except this particular black hair had been on that swatch before I—or my sleeve—had touched it.

That stray bit of hair could have come from anybody, at any time. Anybody at all. It could have been there for years. It could have come from Keith himself—the man had made pet clothes, after all.

Or it could have come from somebody who'd been searching Keith's apothecary cabinet for something.

Did the Gilroys have a black cat, I wondered?

Did Alan and Tracey Howell have one back home?

Chapter Nine

WHEN I REJOINED the funeral reception, I went on a little gossip tour, from the kitchen where my old boss Gretchen sat with her husband, to the corner of plaidville Paul stood in. Gretchen and Barry wanted to know all about notation knives, and I was delighted to oblige them. People usually got all glassy-eyed and yawny when I delivered history lectures at social events. Being invited to give one was a refreshing change.

But despite being in her eighties (ten years her husband's senior, the minx), and having lived in Bryd Hollow all her life, Gretchen looked at me funny when I asked if she knew of any royal lineage on the Howells' part. "Did Keith strike you as a noble sort of person?"

"Well, no. But I heard something along those lines, and you're my best source on the old families."

She shrugged. "I must have been almost twenty years older than Keith, and almost a decade younger than his parents. I never knew any Howells better than to say hello and comment on the weather. And occasionally get annoyed with Keith, rest his soul, but who didn't?"

Paul wanted to talk about something else entirely. He shook his head at me as I made my way over to him, lips pressed in a thin line. "Breaking poor Roark's heart, I see. You are so mean."

I blinked at him. "I ... what?"

He nodded across the room, where Ruby and Roark were talking to Carrie. (Who was Ruby's niece. Small towns.) "He waved to you when you walked by just now, and you totally ignored him."

"He did not wave."

"He absolutely waved."

"Then it was to somebody else. We barely know each other. I don't even know his first name."

Paul laughed, then frowned when he saw I wasn't laughing with him. "That wasn't a joke?"

"What would be funny about that?"

"Nothing, if you meant it to be a joke. I was just laughing to be polite." He smirked. "But it's very funny now that I know you don't know why it's funny. His first name is Roark, dummy."

"Really?"

"Roark McGinty."

Weird, I'd never heard Roark referred to as anything other than Roark. But that did clear up a few things. "So that's why he looks at me funny when I call him Officer Roark. It'd be like if I called you Accountant Paul."

Paul laughed at me a little more, while I denied having seen Roark make any gestures whatsoever as I walked by. (Truth be told, I hadn't even seen Roark as I walked by. Or Ruby and Carrie, for that matter.) This was all interrupted by Carrie, coming over to say hello to me.

"Tell her Roark waved at her, when you were over there with him just now," Paul said to his wife.

"He did," Carrie said. "Looked kind of disappointed that you didn't notice. *And* he was asking about you."

"All right, you two, enough with Roark and the waving. If you're trying to set me up, let's just nip that in the bud right now." In hopes of changing the subject, I gestured toward Carrie's head. "You look great, by the way."

"Thank you." Carrie flipped a couple of her new braids off her shoulder. "But why no setup? Roark's a super nice guy."

"I'm sure he is, but I'm not ready to date. I ... uh ... just got out of a serious relationship." *Three years ago.*

Paul gave me a curious look. We'd been out of touch for a few years before he got me (or more accurately, his wife got me) a job in Bryd Hollow, and he hated missing out on personal details. "Not the college boyfriend still?"

"Brian," I said with a nod. "We did start dating in college, but we were together a long time." *Just not as recently as I'm implying.*

"What happened?" Carrie asked.

He felt that my getting shot in the chest and almost dying made me "no fun anymore." I waved a hand vaguely. "It just didn't work out."

"Well, you don't sound too broken up about it," said Paul.

Are you kidding me? The two bullets I took were

almost worth it for the one I dodged. But I knew where this was going. "I'm fine, but that doesn't mean I'm ready for something new. Besides, I came to Bryd Hollow for a fresh start. The last thing I need is a bunch of exes lying around." I elbowed Paul. "You're more than enough."

"Listen to you." Carrie had one of the most melodious and charming laughs I'd ever heard. That didn't mean I appreciated it at that exact moment. "Not one date, and you've already got poor Roark in the *ex* bin."

I shrugged. "He's not the one."

"But how do you know," she asked, "when you haven't even given him a chance?"

"I just know."

"Uh-huh." Carrie gave me a hard look. "So, where is Percy today?"

I ignored both the awkward transition and the implication in her face. Percy Baird was (probably) not the one, either. Dimples or no dimples, I really didn't need my nice, settled new life mucked up with romantic complications.

Whether I *wanted* it mucked up with romantic complications was a harder question, but I figured I had enough going on without throwing a lot of self-reflection into the mix.

Paul snickered. "Off with his high school sweetheart, maybe?"

"Is that what she is?" I asked, even though I obviously knew that was what she was. What I really wanted to know was whether she was anything more than that— like maybe his today sweetheart. Other than a quick wave across the graveyard this morning, I hadn't seen Percy since the day we came to this very house to give the Howells a pie. It was unusual for us to go that long without walking Plant. Or at least talking.

Paul seemed to grasp my true question. "As far as I know, that flame has not yet been rekindled." He gave me an impish look. "Although you never know. She was his first love, I'm told."

"She definitely was." Carrie pursed her lips and shook her head. "I was only a year behind them in school, and I am here to tell you, they were gross."

Given their predilection for gross nicknames, this did not surprise me, but I decided to keep that thought to myself.

"Maybe so," said Paul, "but I guess her family's not averse to reliving the grossness. To hear Bonnie talk, you'd think she was a Baird-in-law already."

I didn't think much of that word *already*. I sniffed. "Well, I don't know where he is. He was at the service, though, so he must be around here someplace."

"Maybe his mother can tell us," said Carrie, waving across the room. The friendly tornado that was Mrs. B was upon us a second later.

"Hello, hello!" she chirped at Carrie and Paul, with a hug for the former. "*Love* the new hair." She turned to me. "Yours *too*, Minerva! What did you do to it?"

Not a thing. It was still the same boring, too straight chestnut. "It might be an inch longer, maybe?"

"Well I think you look *adorable*!" Mrs. B embraced me like a daughter, as if she'd never kicked me out of a police station, and then her house.

I decided to follow suit, and disregard the previous fall entirely. "Thank you, Mrs. B, it's so nice to see you. I wish it were under less sad circumstances."

She looked blank for a second, like maybe she wasn't accustomed to thinking of funerals as sad occasions, before returning to her exclamations in full force. "Oh! Yes, of course, sad. *Very* sad! I'm told he was *murdered*!"

"Yes, I'm afraid so."

Mrs. B patted my shoulder. "But you'll be seeing me under *happy* circumstances soon, right? You're coming to brunch this weekend?"

"Yes ma'am, thank you for the invitation. I'm looking forward to it."

She shifted her smile back to Carrie and Paul. "And you two as well, yes?"

"Wouldn't miss it," said Paul.

"We're so happy for Elaine and Phil," Carrie added.

"Oh, me *too*!" Mrs. B agreed. "They're so—Oh! Look at *you*, Brooke!"

I turned to see Percy approaching, with Brooke Digby in tow. Mrs. B immediately transferred her enthusiasm to her son's first (and possibly grossest) love, and spent several minutes telling Brooke how wonderful she looked, and how wonderful she was, before insisting she, too, come to brunch that weekend. "And I didn't see you at the service! Were you there?"

"No, my father and I just got here," said Brooke. "We weren't sure how welcome we would be, to tell you the truth. So we decided to just pop by, offer our condolences, and go."

"Not *welcome*!" Mrs. B put her hand to her chest. "Don't be *silly*. I'm sure Alan wouldn't—"

Whatever kind thing she was about to say about Alan Howell was belied by the man himself, shouting loud enough for the whole house to stop what they were doing.

"... think I'm going to tolerate spying in my own house? At my father's funeral?"

"For heaven's sake, Alan!" a female voice replied, nearly as loudly. "I wasn't upstairs, I was sitting on the steps because there was no room anyplace else! You've stuffed this place to the gills to give the impression that somebody, anybody is mourning your father!"

Reasoning that it must be my duty as the funeral's (partial) planner to bear witness to any unpleasant scenes, and not at all because I was as bad a gossip as anybody, I stepped past Paul and craned my neck to get a look at the foyer. The object of Alan's ire was Jana Towe, who stood at the bottom of the stairs with her husband Milton and Ron Digby.

"*You're* not mourning him, that's for sure!" Alan shot back. "So why are you even here?" He rounded on the men to include them in his tirade. "The three of you came to *gloat*, is my guess. That, and to sponge some free food and booze."

"Alan." Tracey appeared at his side. "There's no need to raise your voice. Nobody is gloating."

"They're glad he's dead!" Alan turned to his wife, jabbing a finger at her. "And I'm a hundred percent correct about the booze, by the way, especially in Milton's case."

Milton, who had a reputation as something of a hothead (and a drunk, if you want the truth), advanced on Alan, fists clenched. Jana yanked him back, while Tracey kept speaking to her own husband in soothing tones.

The soothing did no good. Alan jerked away from her and shouted a slew of colorful words that all amounted to *get out*. These were punctuated by a cacophony of cockatiel support from above.

"AND NOW YOU'VE WOKE THE BIRD!" Alan thundered, as if Milton had been the one shouting.

Apparently that pushed the noise beyond Brooke's limit. "See what I mean?" She gave Mrs. B a quick hug. "It was lovely to see you, Mrs. B, but I need to go rescue my dad. Love to Elaine."

"Hope we'll see you on Sunday!" Mrs. B called after her, but all she got in return was a quick wave over the shoulder.

Percy touched my elbow and leaned down to whisper in my ear. "Great job with the arrangements." With a parting squeeze of my shoulder, he followed Brooke.

That was it? No attempt to break the tension with a lame joke or a terrible pun? Who was this guy?

Brooke and Percy collected Ron and eased him out the door. The Towes followed shortly, but much less quietly. I could hear Milton shouting insults at Alan all the way to his car.

It seemed that Bryd Hollow's ill will toward Keith Howell had not been satisfied by his death. It had simply been transferred to his son.

Not that you could especially blame them.

"He's a treat, isn't he?" Ruby came to stand beside me, nodding in the direction of the door.

"And by *he* do you mean Milton, or Alan?" I asked.

She snorted. "I wouldn't want to spend a day off with either of them, now that you mention it."

I wondered who Ruby did spend her days off with. She wasn't married. (I'd heard from Paul that she was, in fact, twice divorced, from exes who didn't make their homes in Bryd Hollow.) Carrie? Carrie's parents?

I didn't know who her friends were—it was hard to picture her relaxing—but I knew she didn't count me among them. If she'd come over to talk to me, it wasn't for idle chatter. "Any word on the knife?" I asked.

"Several words, actually. And some notes." She held up her phone, which she'd clearly already prepped, because all she had to do was press a button. The sound of a piano rose up, playing a few bars of music. "Do you recognize that tune?"

I shook my head. "Can you play it again?"

She did, and I leaned down to listen more closely. But that only made me shake my head again.

"Sounds Renaissance, maybe? Like maybe a choir should be singing it." I bit my lip. "But I know nothing about music or music history. I don't know whether I think it's Renaissance because I really think it, or because I'm thinking about the notation knife, which is a Renaissance thing. Assuming that's the music from the knife?"

Ruby nodded. "Troy DeWitt translated it and recorded it on his piano for me. But we haven't been able to place the song."

"I'm sorry I couldn't be more help."

"I figured it was a long shot, but it never hurts to ask." Ruby tucked her phone back into the pocket of her black trousers. "It might not matter anyway."

"Why's that?"

"I believe the knife's a fake, just like you said it would be."

Just like I said it would be—because of course I'd said that, because of course it was fake.

But I was still disappointed. Wouldn't that have been something, if it had gone the other way. A real notation knife. (*In the flesh*, Percy would have said. *So to speak, har har.* Then when I didn't laugh, he would have explained that he meant it'd been used to stab somebody, because Percy Baird did not get that explaining jokes only made them even less funny.)

"You're certain?" I asked.

Ruby tilted her hand back and forth. "I guess I can't say *certain* yet. I've sent it to some big-shot professor at Chapel Hill for confirmation. But that's just a formality. Basil had a look at it for me when he got back to town."

"And Basil could tell it was fake just by looking at it?" Nothing against Basil, who was a fine antiques dealer, but something like this seemed a little out of his depth.

"Apparently it's not a very good fake," Ruby said. "Not only does he not think it's hundreds of years old, he thinks it was made recently."

I frowned at that. "How recently?"

"Don't know. He said metal's really hard to date, even by the best experts. But he seemed sure it was modern, anyway."

"But that doesn't make sense. Alan said it was an

heirloom. People usually use that word for something that's been around for generations."

"And I'm sure he thought it was," Ruby said with a shrug. "Keith could've lied. Or maybe Keith thought so too, and it was Del Howell who lied to *his* son. Like I told you, Basil couldn't give me an exact year on this thing. Who knows where it started."

I looked over at Alan Howell, who was a few feet away now, talking to a small group of people and swigging craft beer out of a bottle. "You're right, of course."

"I usually am. What am I right about this time?"

"About somebody believing it was an heirloom." I cocked my head. "It doesn't really matter if the knife is real. What matters is that somebody thought it was real."

Beer he might or might not have been able to afford. "Or that somebody thought they could pass it off as real."

Chapter Ten

SNICK LEANED back in his chair and fed a piece of fresh sausage to Plant, who lay behind our table on the ballroom floor. "So, tell us all the gossip from town."

Presuming this directive was for me and not Plant, I raised my eyebrows at him. "You think I have gossip you two don't?"

"We haven't been allowed out of the house for a week!" Dante protested. An enormous man with a ponytail and heavily tattooed arms, the Bairds' new(ish) chef looked more like a biker. But he seemed to fit right in with small-town life.

Unfortunately for him, and for Snick, Mrs. B's "little brunch" for Elaine and Phil had turned out to be seventy guests big, hence the tables set up in the ballroom, the only indoor space that could hold them all. Snick and Dante had pulled the whole thing together themselves.

As a reward for their hard work, Mrs. B had hired some kids from town to handle the service, leaving them free to be guests now that the food was all prepared and things had gotten rolling. The three of us (and Plant) had found an out-of-the-way table on the darker and colder, and therefore quieter, side of the old room, where we could enjoy the fruits of Dante's labor.

"We might not mind a week's worth of overtime, under normal circumstances," Snick said. "But I'm assuming this was an eventful week, what with Keith Howell's funeral and all."

"You've got that right," I said. "His son Alan kicked the Towes and the Digbys out. Oh, and the Gilroys. I helped with that one."

Snick's pale brows shot up. "You're kidding me. Tell us everything."

"There might be taffy in it for you," Dante added. "I made some yesterday."

My jaw dropped. "You *made* taffy?"

"I was trying out a few little confections for Elaine," he said with a shrug. "She's obsessed with candy."

"I didn't know that. I don't think I've ever seen her eat any." I enjoyed this tidbit of information; she was already almost as into the fries at Deirdre's as I was. Add candy to that, and she and I were practically sisters.

Not that I wanted to be her sister, mind. Not in any in-law sort of way. That wasn't what I was thinking at all.

"That's because her father wouldn't let her have it," said Snick. "Even as an adult. You know how Clifford was. She's loosened up a lot since he died."

I studied the happy couple, who stood across the room surrounded by admirers. "Phil's definitely been good for her. Do you know she hasn't gone the least bit bridezilla on me? She's so calm and reasonable." I rolled my eyes. "Especially compared to Bonnie Digby."

"Give it time," said Snick. "I don't know that she's changed *that* much."

"She was never *that* bad." I patted Dante's hand. "And she got Dante to make taffy."

"Well, her and you," said Dante. "Snick told me you'd be super disappointed if I didn't add it to the list. I should warn you though, she didn't think much of it, so this may be the last batch. She's not as into the chewy stuff."

So much for sisterhood. "But the chewy stuff is the best. Soft, fluffy." I closed my eyes and mimicked a euphoric sigh. "What does she like, crunch?"

"Loves crunch," Dante agreed.

"Weirdo. I'll be happy to take the taffy off your hands." I paid his stated price for it, giving him and Snick a full account of the funeral reception, as well as my visit to the Howell house a few days earlier.

"So, who do we like for Keith's murder?" Dante asked when I finished.

"Well ... lots of people had gripes against Keith. Ollie Gilroy hated him, and he was the one who found the body, so you'd have to consider him. *And* he was snooping around at the funeral," I added, disregarding the fact that I'd done the same. I lowered my voice. "And Alan got here awfully fast, after Ruby called him."

"Meaning what?" Snick leaned forward. "Meaning he might have been here the whole time, murdering his father?"

I shrugged. "Maybe Alan wanted to sell the knife,

and Keith wouldn't let him have it. It would have been priceless, if it were real. Which incidentally it isn't. But maybe somebody thought they could sell it as real."

Snick gave Plant another piece of sausage. "I heard Ruby called you in as an expert witness over this knife."

"Isn't an expert witness for a trial?"

He waved this away. "Whatever, you know what I mean. What's the story with the knife?"

"Well, I'm no expert, but I know enough to know it's a weird thing to kill somebody with." I gave them my mini-lecture on notation knives, which I'd had a lot of practice with in recent days. I was pretty sure I'd delivered it a half dozen times at the funeral.

"And it was Keith's own knife?" Dante asked. "The killer didn't bring it?"

"It was Keith's," I said. "Family heirloom, according to Alan."

Dante tilted his chair back and crossed his arms. "Then Keith and the killer had to be fighting over it. That's the only reason you'd kill somebody with their own knife, right? I mean if you went there with the intent to kill him, you'd bring a weapon."

I nodded. "My favorite theory is that the killer was there to steal the knife, and Keith caught them in the act, leading to the struggle."

"Or," said Snick, "maybe it's easier to kill a guy with his own knife than to bring something with you that can be traced back to you." He shook his head, looking disappointed. "You guys would make *terrible* murderers."

Dante ignored him, clearly warming up to the subject of the knife. "But you say the knife isn't real?"

"They're still waiting on expert confirmation," I said. "But Ruby's pretty sure it's not, because Basil's pretty sure it's not. And speaking for myself, I can't think where the Howells would get a thing like that. Percy says they claim some connection to British monarchs, specifically the Tudors, but I haven't been able to find out any more about that. Alan's not exactly chatty."

I drummed my fingers against the table. "Although you know, maybe he's not the only one I could ask. Percy mentioned in passing that Keith's mother is still alive and living in the county someplace." I'd almost forgotten—probably because Alan had never once mentioned his grandmother.

"Dot," said Snick.

"That's her name?"

He nodded. "Dorothea Howell."

"Any idea why she wouldn't have been at the funeral?" I asked.

"Therein lies the hole in your ask-Dot plan." Snick tapped the side of his head with his forefinger. "She's maybe not all there. Keith shipped her off a few years ago after she almost set the house on fire."

"His house?"

"Well, her house, really. That's the house Keith grew up in. But yeah. I don't know if it's dementia or what, but she probably can't tell you much."

"Might be worth a try, though." Dante gave me an encouraging nod. Apparently the whole knife-and-Tudor carriwitchet had captured his imagination as much as it had mine.

"Might be worth going to see her anyway," said Snick. "Dot was a treat, you'd love her. Everyone loved her. I used to take her for a stroll around that little park across Diligence Street once in a while, when she lived here."

I laughed at this. Being kind to little old ladies wasn't exactly Snick's style. "You went into town specifically to take her for walks?"

"No, no, that wasn't how Dot operated. She found you in town and took *you* for a walk." He pitched his voice throatier and more feminine, and affected a Southern accent. "Young man, you look strapping enough. Take my arm and help an old lady grow even older, will you?"

I laughed again. "She does sound like a treat."

"Nothing like her son," said Snick. "I gather he took after the father, but I never met him."

Having gone too long, in his opinion, between pieces of sausage, Plant lumbered to his feet and rested his head on Snick's leg.

"Don't you give him another thing," I told Snick, before looking at Dante. "It doesn't offend you, seeing a dog eat the food you worked so hard on?"

In answer (and in direct defiance of my instructions), Dante tossed Plant a sizable piece of waffle, which the latter caught. "Why should it? He probably appreciates it as much as anyone here."

I pursed my lips at Plant, who was chomping both noisily and messily. "He certainly appreciates it, I'll give you that."

Snick followed my gaze, then pulled a face at the spot

of drool that had just fallen onto his pants. "Maybe a little more than I do."

"You're the one who started feeding him at the table," I pointed out. "You knew the consequences would involve drool. So on these walks you took with Dot, she never said anything to you about, say, Henry Tudor?"

"Somehow that never came up, no. Henry Gilroy, now him she had a few things to say about."

"Any relation to Ollie Gilroy?" I asked.

"Uncle or something, I think. Ollie got the house from Henry."

"So Henry fought with Dot and her husband, and now Ollie fights with Keith? Or Alan now, I guess."

"Circle of life," Snick said. "I bet they were fighting about the exact same things, too."

I shook my head. "Does anybody in Bryd Hollow have any *new* problems?"

"You're one to talk." Snick waved at me. "Henry Tudor this and Renaissance knife that. None of that is exactly new."

"Well, the knife is almost certainly new," I pointed out. "It's just a copy of something old. But you know ..." I chewed at my thumbnail, wishing I had a piece of that taffy now. Taffy always helped me think. "*Why?*"

I looked at Dante, then Snick, but neither of them looked like he particularly understood the question, much less had an answer. "I mean, of all the things, right? There are way easier things to forge, and way, way easier things to sell. Why would the Howells have a fake *nota-*

tion knife? Why would they even know what a notation knife is? And then it ends up in Keith's eye?"

I pointed from one man to the other. "I am telling you guys, fake or not, that knife is the key to all of this."

"You're *still* talking about that knife?"

I turned to find Percy grinning down at me, but my return smile was somewhat dimmed by the presence of Brooke at his side. Percy introduced her to Snick and Dante before dropping to the floor to greet Plant, whose tail was thumping so hard there was some chance of it breaking right off.

"Oh, you're the new George," said Brooke, nodding at Snick. "Nice to meet you."

Percy looked up at her with a huff. "George retired years ago. Snick is actually the second George since George."

She rolled her eyes at him. "And I'm expected to know this how? I haven't been home much since college."

"Yeah." Percy gave her a look I could only describe as wistful. "I noticed."

"So Brooke," I interrupted, then immediately regretted it, since I had no idea what to say to her. "I"—inspiration struck just in time—"was so sorry about what happened the other day. I hope your father's recovered."

She gave me a tight look. "What do you mean?"

"The funeral. Alan was awful."

"Oh, that! Yeah. We've come to expect that kind of thing from the Howells. We wanted to drop in to be respectful and neighborly, you know, but ..." She shrugged. "No big loss. I certainly didn't mind leaving."

"I heard about the Howells' grudge against the Towes," I said, "and the whole bottomless barrel of boys thing. But what's their big gripe against the Digbys?"

"Well, for one thing, Molly Towe, the witch who laid that curse on them?" Brooke switched to a stage whisper, an impish glint in her eye. "She was a Digby."

"Really?" Percy and I said at the same time.

"Oh yeah," said Brooke. "She was only a Towe by marriage. And that marriage apparently only happened because she was a witch, and stole some Howell girl's sweetheart away."

"Huh," said Percy. "I always thought it was something with your grandparents."

Brooke laughed. "You weren't wrong. My grandparents hated Keith's parents. I almost forgot about that."

"Why did they hate Keith's parents?" I asked.

"Some high school rivalry between my Grandma June and Dottie. Cheerleading or something." Brooke waved. "I can't keep up, to be honest. But I'm sure it was something stupid."

"Maybe I can ask Dottie about that too." I smiled over at Dante. "Trade more gossip for taffy, if you don't mind it being fifty years old."

Dante crossed his arms in mock offense. "But I suppose you'd think yourself ill-used if I gave you fifty-year-old taffy."

It was the sort of silly joke Percy would normally have enjoyed, but he was frowning. "What do you mean, ask Dottie?"

"I'm thinking about going to see her," I said. "She might be able to tell me a little more about the Howell family tree, since Alan wasn't very forthcoming."

"Why do you need to know about their family tree?" Brooke asked.

Percy answered for me. "She's curious about that old knife." He shook his head at me. "I don't know about bugging Dottie with that, though. She isn't well."

"So I hear," I said. "Still. You don't think it's worth a try?"

"I think you should leave a sick old woman alone," Brooke said. Despite the fact that nobody had asked for her thoughts on the matter.

I blinked at her. "I wasn't going to interrogate the woman. I thought maybe she would appreciate a visitor. Her family seems to have abandoned her. And she sounds delightful."

"She was delightful," said Brooke, "and now she isn't well. Percy's right, leave Dottie alone."

That wasn't quite what Percy had said, but possibly deliberately, he was now too occupied with rubbing Plant's belly to clarify his view on the matter.

Not that either his view or Brooke's was required, what with me being a grown autonomous adult and all. I gave Brooke a stiff nod and changed the subject to where Elaine and Phil were going to live.

(This turned out to be a long story, the upshot of which was that they were building a new house, tucked away in the mountains not far from Bryd Hollow. Family policy was to pass Baird House to a new generation of Bairds upon the marriage of the oldest child to bear the name. Gwen and Tristan were both older, but Gwen wanted nothing to do with her family, and Tristan would likely never marry. Which meant Elaine could have had the house, had she chosen to keep her name. Except it turned out Phil didn't want to live there, so after some arguing with her intended, Elaine had decided to change her name and move out. To hear Snick tell it, said arguing had been somewhat dramatic.)

Engrossing as it was, this account of Elaine's issues did not distract me from my own. Namely, that if Brooke Digby thought withholding her permission was reason enough for me to not do a thing, she was sorely mistaken. Before she'd butted in with her opinions, I'd been leaning toward paying Dorothea Howell a visit.

Now I was positively determined to.

HONESTLY, even if I hadn't been interested in her family—or irritated with Brooke—I would have wanted to visit Dottie. The poor woman seemed completely forgotten. Neither her grandson nor his wife had so much as mentioned her. Nobody had even bothered to bring her to her own son's funeral.

Putting my intent into practice took a bit of doing, though. Snick didn't know where she lived, and I wasn't about to ask Percy about her again. Instead I sat on my couch the afternoon after the Baird brunch, Plant sprawled across my lap, laptop balanced on his back, and started calling long-term care facilities, assisted living apartments, and senior communities to ask if I could speak with Dottie Howell. Best case, somebody would let me, which would be a convenient way to make sure she didn't mind if I came. You know, as opposed to allowing a Digby, her mortal enemy, to decide for her.

Worst case, they wouldn't even tell me whether or not they had a patient by that name. Which was what happened with two of the first six places I called. The other four told me they had no such resident, which was at least good for eliminating them.

It was hard to interpret the marketingspeak of the seventh place I found, Starlight Senior Living *(Make the twilight years bright!)*, but it appeared to be some sort of middle ground between a nursing home and independent senior living, which was promising. If it wasn't a medical facility, they might be allowed to be a little more free with information.

And so they were. The receptionist put me on hold for several minutes before somebody else picked up and told me that Dottie was at water therapy, but that she had most weekday afternoons free except Thursdays, and I was welcome to come any other day before eight.

Perfect. I just so happened to have Wednesday off, in exchange for working a conference on Saturday. I could go then. Stunned by my luck to have been given such a wealth of information so easily, I thanked the woman profusely.

"Oh, no problem at all," she said. "I'm happy to encourage visitors for Dot. I've only been here three months, but I don't think she's had a single one in all that time."

So nobody had told her that Keith was dead? Maybe they couldn't; maybe her condition or mental state wouldn't allow for it. But either way, the fact that she was just as abandoned as I'd feared only strengthened my resolve to see her.

I looked down at Plant, whose bony elbows were digging into my thighs. Surely with his sunny disposition and charming good looks, he could do a little moonlighting as a therapy dog. Therapy dogs visited nursing homes all the time, didn't they?

"One other thing, while I have you," I said to the woman on the phone. "Do you think Dottie would enjoy a visit from a friendly dog? If you even allow that?"

She said she was sure Dottie would be delighted to see us both.

I hoped she was right.

Chapter Eleven

I was glad I'd brought Plant, if only for the moral support as I approached Starlight Senior Living, which did not look like the sort of place that would make your twilight years bright. I'm honestly not sure how to describe it, other than to say it looked like it came straight out of a movie. And not a comedy.

For one thing, it was up high, which meant a lot of twisty roads. Not that that was unusual—I lived in the mountains now, I'd gotten used to twisty roads—but it didn't help the place look more inviting, sitting up there on its own. Sprawling and tall, it might once have been a hotel.

The building was dark brown brick, with a black roof, a lot of chimneys, and no garden or greenery at all. The trees that lined its tiny drive wouldn't be budding for another month yet, lending to the sparse and fore-boding appearance.

"Plant," I said as I parked my car, "I'm pretty sure this place is haunted."

Plant licked my ear in what I assumed was agreement.

But maybe haunted was okay. I'd come to ask about the past, after all. Maybe the ghosts would have something useful to say.

Fortunately for the residents and staff, the lobby was much more cheerful. The hotelesque feel continued here, but it was more Ritz than Bates, with expensive but tasteful furniture. There were flowers everywhere; I wondered who their florist was.

I also wondered who was paying for a place like this for Dottie Howell.

Despite how easily they'd parted with the information that Dottie lived here, they clearly took security at least somewhat seriously. A large sign told me I needed to check in to proceed beyond that point, and a security guard was leaning against the wall near the elevators.

After taking my ID and entering my name into the visitor log, the friendly woman behind the desk gave me a Guest sticker for my sweater, then called an even friendlier woman to take me and Plant upstairs.

Woman number two introduced herself as Lia as she led me to the elevators. "I'm one of the caretakers here."

"Is that like a nurse, or a doctor?" I asked, and nearly added *or a psychologist*. The place did look like an old-timey asylum, at least from the outside.

"None of the above," said Lia. "We do have nurses and physical therapists who work here full time, but our residents don't need round-the-clock medical care or anything like that. They just need varying degrees of support. Each caretaker has a block of rooms that we coordinate services for, and Dot's one of mine."

So more like a concierge, then. Interesting. Everybody in Bryd Hollow had acted like Dottie was an invalid, but how bad off could she be, if she was living semi-independently into her nineties? Which couldn't have been too far off her age, since Gretchen had surmised she was close to a decade younger than Dot.

Lia got into an elevator and held the doors open while I employed a generous portion of liver treats to coax Plant (who hated elevators) inside. "I think we spoke on the phone, by the way," she said. "I recognize your voice."

"Oh! Yours sounded familiar, too." She was the one who'd told me that Dottie hadn't been getting visitors. "You mentioned starting pretty recently. Do you like it here?"

"Oh I *love* it." Lia punched the button for the eighth floor. "You see a lot of nightmarish stuff about old folks' homes, mostly in bad movies, but everyone here is *great*." Something about her enthusiasm reminded me of Mrs. B.

The eighth floor hallway went right or left from the bank of elevators, with a sign on the wall pointing left for rooms 800-849, and right for rooms 850-899. Exactly one hundred rooms? The Starlight website had called them apartments, but I didn't see how they could fit a hundred full-sized apartments per floor. The building was big, but it didn't seem that big.

Then again, they probably didn't let some—or maybe most—of their residents have kitchens. Snick had mentioned Dottie almost setting her house on fire.

I didn't know which way we wanted, so I waited for

Lia to lead the way. But she hesitated after the elevator doors closed. "So, how well do you know Dot?"

"I don't know her at all," I confessed. I was here now; surely Lia wouldn't just decide I wasn't allowed to see the woman, not when she'd been so excited about her getting a visitor. She was no Brooke Digby. And anyway, she would find out soon enough, if she was going to introduce me to Dottie. I wasn't going to try to convince a confused old woman that she knew me.

"I live in her home town," I said. "I'm working on a history project, and I wanted to ask her a few questions."

Lia didn't seem the least bit disturbed by this information. "Well, she'll love that." She reached down and scratched the top of Plant's head. "And she'll love you, won't she?"

Plant wiggled his back end in affirmation that Dottie would indeed love him.

"But I don't know how well you'll be able to trust the answers she gives you," Lia went on. "Dot kind of lives in her own world."

I nodded. "I heard she might be confused."

"On a good day." Lia started down the left hallway. "The reason I asked how well you know her is, I don't know if anybody warned you not to call her Mrs. Howell?"

"Um. No?"

"Yeah, she's kind of ... regressed, you might call it. She gets agitated when she's confronted with the fact that it isn't 1957 anymore, and you do not want to deal with an agitated Dot. We call her Miss McGinty, if we have to get formal. That was her maiden name."

"Great, I'll do that. Thank you."

Odsbodikins. I'd been prepared for Dot to have some difficulties, but if she didn't even remember she was a Howell, how much could I reasonably expect her to tell me about their family history?

Assuming she bore some relation to His-First-Name-Is-Roark McGinty, I wondered how close it was. Maybe she was his great aunt or something, and he would remember some old stories she'd told him when he was a little boy. And one of those stories would happen to be about her husband's Tudor lineage.

Yeah. Seemed like a long shot.

It was too late to worry about it; here we were at room 824. Lia knocked and waited for permission to come in, which was granted in a reedy yet girlish voice.

Plant's lead firmly in hand, lest he get overexcited about a new place, I followed Lia into a small but luxurious sitting room, with doors to the right and left and a bank of windows straight ahead. The windows showed a lovely view of the mountains. Dottie Howell certainly had a nicer place than I did. A nicer place than the house she'd come from, for that matter.

The woman herself was sitting in a chair in front of a television that wasn't turned on, dressed in a pair of pink floral pajamas. She was a slip of a thing, with silky white hair and a delicate face that I had no doubt could have launched a thousand ships in her day. Despite both her age and the warnings about her mental state, her big, round eyes looked alert and clear.

I pulled Plant closer to my side when I saw a cinnamon-colored cat curled up on her lap, surprised that Lia had failed to mention this detail. Thankfully, Plant was fine with cats. But who knew if the cat was fine with him?

"Dottie, you have a visitor, if you're up for it." Lia took my elbow and led me forward. "This is Minerva Biggs. And her dog, Plant. I know how you love dogs. I thought he might be a treat for you."

"An animal named Plant?" Dottie asked. "Well that's cheeky of you, isn't it? Bring him over and let's have a look at him."

I led him closer to her chair, where he stretched out his neck to sniff the cat. The cat, in turn, opened one eye, decided we weren't worth disturbing his or her nap for, and closed it again.

Meanwhile, Dottie peered at me. "I don't know you." Her tone was firm, but not unfriendly or suspicious. Like the question of my familiarity had been a puzzle to solve, neither good nor bad.

"No, you don't," Lia agreed, before I could answer. "She's from your home town, though, and she wanted to chat with you about the town history."

"Oh!" Dottie gave me a radiant smile that displayed a set of obviously false teeth, so white they were almost blue. Despite the dentures, that smile made her look twenty—if not sixty—years younger. "That does sound like fun." She transferred her sunny look to Lia. "Are we allowed to have tea?"

"Sure, I'll have some sent up," Lia said. So the place didn't have a kitchenette, or so much as a hot pot. "Do you want cookies?"

"Do I want cookies." Dottie looked at me and rolled

her eyes. "You'll notice I did not say that like a question. Because it's not a real question, is it?"

I smiled back. "I suppose not."

"Yes," Dottie said to Lia. "We would very much like cookies, thank you."

"I'll leave you two to it, then." Lia gave me a thumbs up and left, while Dottie bent toward the cat's ear, as if to impart some great secret.

"Do you hear that, Miss Havisham? We're to have cookies." She reached out a slender hand for Plant, but couldn't quite reach. She waved at the leash in my hand. "Let the poor boy be, will you?"

Confident that Plant understood this was somebody to be gentle with, now that he'd taken the introductions so calmly, I unclipped the leash and let him get closer to Dottie. "Careful, though," I said. "He'll lick your face if you get it too close to him."

Disregarding this warning, Dottie leaned over Plant, accepted a couple of licks to her cheek, then kissed the top of his head. "Aren't you a lovely boy? I bet you'd like a cookie, too, wouldn't you?"

Plant promptly fell into his most handsome sit, although as far as I knew, he did not know the meaning of the word *cookie*.

"Did I hear correctly that your cat's name is Miss Havisham?" I asked. At the sound of her name, the character in question opened her eyes, but did not raise her head.

"You did," said Dottie. "It's a much more sensible name for a cat than Plant is for a dog."

I laughed. "You're not wrong. So you're a Dickens fan?"

"I have great expectations of my own life," Dottie said proudly. "I'm getting married."

Not as lucid as she looked, then. "Congratulations."

"Thank you. Please, won't you sit?"

I sat at the end of a nearby loveseat, shifting so she could see me as easily as possible. Plant stretched out on the floor between us, while Miss Havisham looked on, twitching her tail in what I interpreted as mild suspicion.

"Who's the lucky man?" I asked.

Dottie gave me a wicked grin, once again vanishing years off her face. "*That* depends on who you ask. I have more than one offer."

"Ah, so you're already way ahead of Miss Havisham, then. She only had the one, and he jilted her."

"Very true, very true. Neither of these boys would jilt me."

"I'm sure they wouldn't."

"I'm definitely going to marry Winston, though," Dottie said with a firm nod. "Del isn't the man for me."

Well, that was interesting. I didn't know who Winston was, but I knew Keith Howell's father had been named Del. "Do you mean Del Howell?"

"Of course I do. I thought you said you were from Bryd Hollow."

"Not from there, but I live there now."

"Oh, I see. I guess you haven't met everyone yet. But he's the only Del in Bryd Hollow."

"So why isn't he the man for you?" I asked. "I

thought the Howells were a prominent family. One of the founding ones."

"They are." She pointed at me. "But so too are the Digbys, if you don't know that yet. And Winston will be a better provider than Del, I think."

So Winston was a Digby. Even more interesting.

Dottie leaned forward and whispered, probably loudly enough for the resident across the hall to hear, "Del is more exciting."

"But Winston is more stable."

"Exactly, exactly. I see you understand!"

"I suspect most of us have had the bad-boy dilemma, at some point or other." I was interrupted by a knock on the door (not that I minded being deprived of the chance to relive my bad-boy days). While I got up to answer it, Plant did a couple of deep-chested *woofs* to be sure whoever was on the other side understood this place was now under his protection.

A young man dressed in jeans and a t-shirt came in, pushing a hotel-style room service cart that held a pot of tea, two old-fashioned china teacups, and a plate of Oreos. I was reminded of Tracey's Oreos, back in the Howell house—the house Dottie had raised Keith in. Now she apparently didn't even remember giving birth to him.

No wonder nobody had brought her to the funeral. She would have been utterly confused.

Plant got up to inspect the new arrival, freeing up the space between the loveseat and Dottie's chair for the tea cart. When the man had wheeled it into place, he gave

Dottie a cheerful greeting, patted Plant's head, and turned to go.

This place really was like a hotel. Should I tip the guy? He didn't pause or anything, like he expected one. Only gave me a wave over his shoulder as he closed the door behind him.

I poured Dottie some tea, trying to think of a way to bring the conversation around to the Tudors and the notation knife, without implying that she ought to know these things because she was herself a Howell.

Well, I guessed I didn't need an elaborate story. Lia had already told her I was working on a history project, and that was true in its way. It would do just fine. "So you must know the Howells pretty well," I said, "if Del proposed to you."

"Oh, yes. Del and I grew up on the same street. We've known one another since we were small." Dottie took a cookie and leaned back, considering as she bit it. "I think I'll marry Winston, though."

"I'm sure you'll choose wisely," I said, which was actually kind of heartbreaking. Did this apparent regression stem from taking the wrong path? Was she living inside her regrets now?

I hoped not, but whatever the reason for Dottie's fantasy world, I decided to indulge the poor woman a bit longer before I got back to my own purpose. "Do you think you'll get married at Tybryd, now that it's open to the public?" I asked.

"Open to the public?" Confusion knit her brow. "Do you mean the tours they do on certain weekends?"

Odsbodikins. Lia had specifically said 1957. Thinking

myself a little too clever, I'd brought up Tybryd opening as a hotel—an event that had occurred in 1954, and would no doubt have been the talk of the town for the next few years—in hopes of helping bring Dottie back to that time.

Except Lia must have gotten the year wrong, because Dottie's face was clouding over.

Chapter Twelve

"Why would I want to get married while touring somebody else's house?" Dottie shifted to the edge of her chair, displacing poor Miss Havisham, who stalked off into the next room with her tail in the air. "What sort of question is that?"

"You're right," I said. "I misspoke. I didn't mean *get married* there, of course. That would be strange, wouldn't it?"

I laughed awkwardly, mostly to buy myself some time. "I meant do you think you'll go there the day of the wedding ... for ... to have pictures taken! You know, in one of the gardens. They're so beautiful, they would make for lovely photos."

That was entirely true. I ought to know, since I regularly arranged shoots for brides and grooms in most of the gardens. And if a thing was entirely true it was also, I decided, an entirely credible thing to say.

Dottie seemed inclined to agree, if hesitantly. "That is

a very interesting idea," she said—but slowly, and her forehead was still as furrowed as could be.

In my desire to reel her in, I made the classic liar's mistake: I kept talking. "You could even ride the ferris wheel in your wedding dress. Now *that* would be a fun picture."

I thought the ferris wheel was a safe topic, as it had originally been built in 1924. Though it had been updated, renovated, and probably downright replaced a time or two for safety reasons, one ferris wheel or another had stood in its place continuously ever since.

But I'd said the wrong thing again. Dottie stood up, looking equal parts confused and furious. "Richard Baird doesn't let the public ride the ferris wheel. Not ever. You ought to know that. Why wouldn't you know that?"

I started to murmur something about not realizing, and being a recent arrival, but Dottie waved a finger at me. "You might be new to Bryd Hollow, but nobody is *that* new." She put her bony hands on her even bonier hips. "Who are you really?"

Plant, bless his heart, sensed the rising tension and came to sit on my foot. Which hurt, but I appreciated the support. I remembered Lia's words as we approached the apartment: *You do not want to deal with an agitated Dot.*

She'd also said Dot got agitated when forced to confront the true year. Which made sense, because the old woman was trembling with indignation as she stood before me and my dog, waiting for us to account for ourselves. Nobody would get this mad about the ignorance of ferris wheel rules. She was mad because my bringing it up reminded her that the public could, indeed, ride the ferris wheel—*now*.

Okay, so put that ferris wheel riding in the context of the early fifties. Think.

How old would Clifford have been then? Too young for my purposes—maybe not even born. But Richard Baird, Clifford's father, was the oldest of several siblings. Who was the youngest?

"Ronnie Baird!" Feeling proud that I'd thought of the name so quickly, and under pressure no less, I got a little overexcited and said it out loud.

The lowlight of this visit was definitely me.

Dottie advanced a couple steps toward the loveseat where I still sat, tiny fists clenched. Plant leaned his head back to look at me and let out a soft, questioning whine, as if perplexed over whether we were actually facing a threat.

I reached out to scratch his neck and murmured, "Its okay. We're fine." I seemed to be more of a threat to Dottie than the other way around.

"You cannot think," she said, lips quivering, "that I'm stupid enough to believe that you're *Ronnie Baird*."

"Of course not, no!" I made my laugh as breezy as I could. "No, you asked who I am, and since you already know my name, I assumed you were looking for more than that. I work for Ronnie Baird. Well, at the moment I do. I'm a history teacher, and he hired me to tutor him."

I leaned forward, put one hand to the side of my mouth, and stage-whispered, "He's *flunking*." I did not mention where Ronnie was doing this flunking, or why I would be tutoring him in Bryd Hollow instead of there, but I hoped these omissions would go unnoticed. I'd barely remembered the guy's name; I had no idea where, or even if, he'd attended college.

It didn't matter; it seemed I'd finally landed on the thing that would defuse Dottie Howell, in the person of Ronnie Baird. She snorted and turned back to her chair, as if she hadn't just looked ready to punch me a second ago. "Ronnie is as dumb as a goat, which is a rude thing to say—about the goat."

She sat back down, chuckling at her joke, but her posture seemed a little stiff yet, and her face looked just a little warier than it had before.

"Anyway," I said, before she had time to punch any more holes in my story, "the ferris wheel thing came from Ronnie. You might be able to ride it by your wedding day."

"Oh?" Dottie frowned. "Why would that be?"

I bit my lip, trying to look coy, which was not a talent of mine. "Can you keep a secret?"

Dottie's eyes lit up. "I've been known to keep a few."

I almost laughed. That wasn't exactly an answer, was it? "Ronnie says his brother Richard is considering moving his family into Baird House, and converting Tybryd into a *hotel*."

She waved a hand, as if shooing me away. "Oh nonsense. He would never!"

"That's what I thought, too. But Ronnie said—"

"Eh, I wouldn't put much stock in anything he says," Dottie cut in, now sounding only mildly interested in a subject that had enraged her just a few moments before. "Besides being an idiot, he's a known liar."

Her eyes widened, perking up again. "I hope you aren't *involved* with him?"

"No, no, nothing like that."

"Good. Because I know it can be tempting, for pretty girls to go after Bairds." She sounded sisterly now. We'd be braiding each other's hair in a minute. "A Baird *seems* like a great catch. But trust me, it's always a mistake. They treat us local girls *awfully*. Good enough for a Saturday night at the diner, but not to marry, if you know what I mean."

Always a mistake. I cleared my throat, and definitely did not think of Percy. "Well, there's nothing going on between me and Ronnie. I'm just his tutor."

"Oh, right. Then you ought to know he's as thick as they come. History, you said?"

"That's right."

Dottie's eyes went a little vague. "A history teacher. Now what was it about that ..." She tapped her chin. "Oh. Lia already told me you're a history teacher, didn't she? That must be it. Or was it a history project?"

"Both," I said, through a sigh of relief. Back to the topic I'd come for, and thank heavens. Straying from it had turned out to be no kindness to Dot. "Although maybe it's more of an antiquities project. That's why I was asking about Del. I'm particularly interested in a knife the Howell family has."

I would have liked to pull out my phone and show her a picture of a notation knife, but I didn't dare. She obviously wasn't living *entirely* in the fifties; the television in front of her was perfectly modern, for one thing. But I didn't know her rules for mixing past and present, and I couldn't risk upsetting her again.

"Now I remember!" Dottie gave me a triumphant smile, probably a lot like the one on my own face when I'd remembered Ronnie Baird's name. "You must be working with that other girl, then."

Other girl? "Which other girl would that be?" I asked.

Had somebody else been asking about the knife? And if so, in which century?

It could have been Ruby, I supposed. But Lia had specifically said that Dot hadn't had any visitors in months. Unless somebody had broken into the building, or scaled the walls and come through Dottie's window, she was probably remembering a conversation from decades ago.

Dottie clasped her hands. "Two professors, and both of you women! How wonderful."

"I didn't realize she'd been here," I said. "You know the knife I mean, then?"

"Of course I know it. It was Henry VIII's knife. The Howells are descended from the Tudors, you know, from the Welsh Tudor line."

My pulse sped up. "I heard something about that. Henry VIII, though? Are you sure?"

"Of course I'm sure. It's one of the reasons I'm not going to marry Del."

I blinked at her. "Because of Henry VIII? Or because of the knife?"

"Henry, of course. They make a big deal out of the

connection. For all I know, cruelty runs in their blood." Dottie straightened her narrow shoulders. "Henry VIII had nine wives, and he chopped the heads off *every one.*"

I resisted the urge to launch into a verbal essay on Henry VIII, starting with the fact that he'd had six wives, and beheaded two. Instead I asked, "How do they know the knife was Henry's? It doesn't seem possible to know for sure. How would distant relations even come by something like that?"

She gave me an impatient look. "I explained all of this to your partner already, can't you just look at her notes? I'm getting very tired."

I felt a surge of guilt; she did look tired. Thanks to me.

I'd have to wrap this up, but asking Dottie in which year she'd received this mysterious visitor would probably be a mistake. Maybe I could identify her another way. "The thing is, she didn't tell me she was coming to see you. I wonder if we're even talking about the same person. What did she look like?"

"Youngish, for a professor. Older than me, of course, but maybe your age. Pretty. She might even have been prettier than you, if it weren't for that scar."

My blood felt like it had just cooled down a good ten degrees. "Scar?"

"No need to be coy about it, I saw it. I notice she tries to cover it with her hair, but I'm very observant." Dottie narrowed her eyes at me, suddenly suspicious again. "Did you give it to her? Is that why you're trying to help her hide it?"

And now my blood was downright frozen. "Was it"

—I touched my cheek at the temple, near the ear—
"around this area? Looked like a burn?"

"Yes, but you know that, don't you? You gave it to
her, didn't you? Was it an accident, at least?" Dottie
looked a little lost now, like maybe I was frightening her.
My heart clenched. This poor woman.

I was a ratbag.

But I wasn't the only one.

"No, of course I didn't give it to her. I ..." I tried to
come up with a story that would satisfy her, but found
my mind was spinning too fast to catch most of my
thoughts. "It was a radiator, when we were kids. Steam."

"You grew up together? And now you work
together? Are you *both* new to Bryd Hollow?" Dottie's
voice got higher and reedier as she spoke.

Plant padded over to her and rested his big head on
her leg, but if he hoped to offer some reassurance, he
missed the mark. Dottie looked at him like a monster had
just fallen into her lap. I wished Miss Havisham would
come out from wherever she'd gone, and comfort her
mistress.

"It's kind of a long story," I said. "But I promise, I
had nothing to do with the scar."

"Are you sisters, is that it?"

"No." I might have been distracted and dumb-
founded, but I had a firm grasp on that particular reality.
"We are not."

I was most definitely not Brooke Digby's sister.

Chapter Thirteen

ODSBODIKINS. Brooke hadn't been worried about the welfare of "a sick old woman" at all. She'd been worried that I would find out she'd already visited that same sick old woman.

Or worried that I would find out whatever it was that Dottie had told her.

That the knife supposedly belonged to Henry VIII? That was all I'd gotten, really. I'd only stayed a little while after the revelation of Brooke's visit, to be sure I wasn't leaving Dottie in a state. She hadn't wanted to talk about Del anymore. She'd wanted to talk about Winston. The one who got away.

Also: the one who was Brooke's grandfather.

Anybody who'd visited Dottie for any length of time would know about her and Winston. Yet Brooke had pretended to be only vaguely aware of the cause of the bad blood between her grandparents and the Howells. Pretended to have almost forgotten there was bad blood at all, no less.

Not to mention that the cause she'd been so vague about was obviously entirely fabricated, to put the focus on her grandmother instead of her grandfather. School-girl fight, my eye.

Brooke really didn't want me to know anything, did she?

Why not?

I drummed my fingers against the steering wheel as I considered this question. Despite it being my day off, I was going straight to Tybryd from Starlight, to see about lightening up my to-do list a bit. Maybe I'd give Plant a nice walk through one of the dog-friendly gardens before dinner. Walking always helped me think.

For once, I hoped I wouldn't run into Percy there. I'd have to tell him all of this. He was in a much better position to figure out what was going on with Brooke than I was. But what was I going to say to him?

So, Perce. Turns out Brooke Digby's a hornswaggler. Think she might be a murderer too?

Did *I* think she might be a murderer?

It was hard to say. I didn't know her very well. And let's face it: where I disliked her, it was for mostly petty reasons stemming from a jealousy I did not want to admit to. I reminded myself of the things about Brooke that didn't fit, like the fact that I'd seen the Digbys' cat, and he was white, not black.

Then again, that dog-or-cat hair in Keith's apothecary cabinet hadn't necessarily come from the killer. Any old snoop could have left it there.

If the Howells thought the knife was real, everybody else who knew about it probably thought so, too. In which case, we were talking about something worth a *lot* of money. And that might be motive enough for anybody.

Based on the conversations I'd had and overheard at Keith's funeral, the knife's existence did not seem to be common Bryd Hollow knowledge. But Dottie had known about it. Had she ever shared that information with Winston? Had he shared it with his granddaughters?

Other than having some nefarious intentions with regard to the knife, why would Brooke go ask Dottie about it—and keep that visit such a secret?

Lia had only been at Starlight a few months, but that would put her there well before Brooke came to town. Well before the knife turned up in Keith Howell's eye, too. And probably before the would-be thief, now murderer, had formed their plans—which they would have needed information about the knife to do.

Given the timing of her arrival, Brooke had most likely seen Dottie after Lia started, which meant she'd snuck in somehow. Lied and said she was visiting somebody else, maybe. Or else attacked a staff member, knocked them out, and stole their clothes and ID badge, like they always did on TV. But probably the first one.

And what about the day of Keith's murder? The Digby girls had darkened my office door just before five. They'd been shopping beforehand (or so they said), but for how long?

I remembered Ruby, the night of the murder, asking for my whereabouts between one and five. If the murderer had killed Keith as early as one, and lived in

Bryd Hollow, they could've been home, in and out of the shower, and out of their house again by two.

What time had Ron shooed Brooke and Bonnie out? And where exactly had they gone?

My many questions about Brooke crowded my head —causing a little ache behind my right eye—until I got to the office, where they were forced to make some space for the question of a band for Elaine's wedding. The orchestra the Bairds used for the ball every year was excellent, but she didn't want to duplicate any of the ball vendors; she wanted her wedding to feel like its own unique event.

Which was not an unusual or especially unreasonable demand, for a bride. But it was a difficult one, in this case, simply because the Bairds already used the best of everything the county had to offer. It was going to be a challenge to find something different, but equally good.

I was going through my sample sound files and videos, contemplating this problem, when I got a text from Ruby: *My guy at Chapel H showed the knife music to a colleague there.*

And? I texted back.

16th cent French song Jouissance Vous Donneray. Ring any special bells?

Off the top of my head, it didn't, but the name sounded vaguely familiar. *Not sure. I'll look it up and let you know if I think of anything that relates.*

Thx. He confirmed knife is fake btw.

Can't say I'm surprised.

I did look it up, as soon as I put my phone back down. I learned that "Jouissance Vous Donneray" was composed by one Claudin de Sermisy; that it was first published in 1528; that it was meant for four voices, and apparently about love; that there was a version of it that had once been used for dancing.

What I did not learn was what it had to do with Keith Howell.

Or with any sort of notation knife, for that matter. It was a secular song. Any notation knife I'd ever heard of featured religious music, a blessing or thanks for the meal the knife was presumably a part of.

That this particular song was on the Howell knife was, I supposed, that much more proof that it was fake. And like Ruby had said, not even a particularly good fake.

I would have liked to keep searching, at least long enough to figure out why I would have heard the name of the song before, when music was definitely not my area of expertise. Or even adjacent to my area of expertise. But I was interrupted by Percy, poking his head (and therefore his dimples) into the office.

I hadn't seen him since the Baird brunch, which meant Plant hadn't seen him since the Baird brunch. I barely got a nod before Percy got down on the floor to accept my dog's exuberant greeting. When Plant finished thoroughly sliming the poor guy's not-even-remotely-poor suit, he grabbed a sample of lace off Sajani's desk and pranced around the room, tail high, with an expression that can only be described as smug.

"That's very nice," Percy assured him.

"*So* nice," I agreed. "Now leave it."

"Dropped in to see Carl, saw the light on in here,"

Percy said, by way of explanation for his presence in the main building. I was unclear on why he thought I required one. "Figured I'd stop and see why you're here so late on your day off."

I glanced at my phone, which informed me it was Past Dinnertime For Dogs. No wonder Plant had been sighing so much. "I'm trying to come up with a short list of potential orchestras or bands for Elaine's wedding. It's a challenge."

Percy flopped down in Sajani's chair. "Carrie James —that's Carrie Kwon, to you—and I were in a band together in high school. Maybe we could find out where the other two are and get back together, as a favor. Since it's for my sister and all."

I laughed. "You were in a what now?"

"Oh yes, we were very good." Percy picked up a pen from Sajani's desk and twirled it between his fingers like a baton. "Especially me. I could've been a famous drummer, if I hadn't been forced so cruelly into the family business."

"Funny, Tristan wasn't forced into the family business. I had the impression you made that choice yourself."

Percy dropped the pen. "Fine. I stank. Did you eat yet?"

"No."

"Come home with me. Phil's coming over for dinner, and he's bringing that new guy he just brought in. You can talk to the happy couple about bands, and Plant can meet the new vet."

He gave Plant's head a vigorous scratch, which led to

Sajani's desk being battered by a tail that would've put an iguana to shame. "You want to meet the new vet, don't you buddy? Of course you do."

"I'll bet he wants to go home and get his dinner more," I said.

"Dante will give him some chicken and rice."

Well, I *did* have business with Elaine. Which was a perfectly good reason to accept the invitation. As opposed to wanting more of Dante's cooking. Or wanting to spend time with Percy.

Or wanting to casually ask him whether he thought his ex—and possibly current—girlfriend might have stabbed a guy in the eye.

"You're sure it won't be a problem for Dante?" I bit my lip. "Or your mother?"

"My mother'll be delighted, and Dante always makes plenty, especially when we have people coming."

"All right then, thank you. I'll meet you there."

"Nah, you can't have wine if you drive." Percy stepped aside so I could get around him and clip on Plant's leash. "Just come with me, and I'll bring you guys home after."

"I can't leave my car here."

"Why not? You have a permit. I'll drive you in tomorrow morning, and then your car will already be here for you to get home."

This seemed like an overly elaborate arrangement, but the Bairds did always serve good wine. And one glass of it really was enough to make driving a poor decision for me.

Plus, it would give me a chance to talk to Percy alone. I thanked him again, and off we went.

"So," I asked as he backed out of his parking space, "will Brooke be there?"

"Where?"

"At dinner."

"Now?"

"Yes, now."

"No, why would she be?"

I shrugged. "No reason. I just thought you two were hanging out a lot." *And also I was just looking for an opening to talk about her.*

"We are when we can. You know, we're old friends. We've known each other since we were little kids, and I haven't seen her in a long time."

"Right. That's what I meant." Well this was awkward. Did he think I was demanding an explanation for the time he spent with Brooke? Did he feel he needed to justify it to me?

"Anyway, she doesn't have a ton of time to hang out. She's working remotely, and her mom ..." Percy sighed. "Things are complicated at their house."

"I got that sense." But I had no details, because Percy had been tight-lipped about it. "Cancer, you said?"

"Yeah." He glanced at me, drumming on the wheel as always. "Terminal. She decided not to do another round of chemo, so they're just sort of ... waiting."

"How awful."

"Yeah, it's sad, I guess."

I stared at him. "You guess?"

"Like I said, it's complicated." Percy shifted in his

seat. "She's not a good mom. Or a good person. You probably didn't notice, but Brooke has a scar, right here." He touched his temple.

"I did notice it, actually." *And so did Dottie Howell.*

"Her mom burned her. This was when we were maybe freshmen in high school? Definitely high school, anyway. Hit her with an iron."

My mouth dropped open. "Did you just say an *iron*? A clothes iron."

"Like one of those little ones, but yeah."

"And did she go to jail for this?"

"Nope. I know they got a visit from somebody who worked for the county, a social worker or whatever. But the whole family backed it being an accident, including Brooke, and nothing came of it."

"An accident?" I huffed. "What, she accidentally walked into an *iron*?"

Percy shrugged. "They were always making excuses for Julie."

"Always? You're saying the iron wasn't an isolated incident?"

"Well, it was by far the worst of them. That I know of, anyway. It was usually smaller things. Borderline things. But Julie Digby was always mean as a snake. And the temper on her ..." Percy drifted off, shaking his head.

"And Ron never put a stop to it?"

He snorted. "I think Ron had it the worst of anybody in that house. You saw them the other day, when he said we were disturbing her. She can't weigh more than eighty pounds at this point, but every one of them is scared of her. Him maybe most of all."

"Odsbodikins," I said, partly to myself. "No wonder you two bonded as kids."

Percy's brow furrowed. "What do you mean?"

"One abusive parent, one who's too terrorized to stop it? Sounds a lot like your family."

Percy's chuckle sounded sincerely befuddled. "What are you talking about? I'll grant you that my father was a ... ratbag, as you would say. But he never beat us with an iron."

"He didn't have to beat you to be abusive."

"Minerva, we were not abused children. You saw how we live and"—Percy gestured vaguely—"everything."

I saw everything, all right. But I resisted the urge to note that you didn't have to be poor to be abusive either, and dropped the subject. Even for a close friend, I'd probably overstepped as it was.

Which was a pity for multiple reasons, not least of which that it had taken us off the topic of Brooke—and I still hadn't found a way to tell Percy she was lying.

Chapter Fourteen

MY DINNER at Baird House had many highlights. Phil Mendoza was a really nice guy. The other vet, whose name turned out to be Charlie, was also a really nice guy. He'd brought his wife with him, and she was a really nice lady.

Mrs. B was, as you might expect, *delighted* to have such *wonderful* guests, and frankly, their dinner table was a whole lot more pleasant when Clifford Baird wasn't presiding over it. Dante's cooking was every bit as fabulous as it had been at brunch, and he even slipped me another little box of taffy that he'd been meaning to ask Percy to bring me.

I spent most of the night talking to Elaine about bands and other wedding ideas. Phil and Charlie doted over Plant as much as Mrs. B and Percy did, and my dog was pretty much in heaven. Especially when he served a heaping bowl of chicken and rice.

The lowlight came when Percy drove me home.

Emboldened by two glasses of wine, I jumped fully

into the topic I'd been so afraid to dip a toe into before. "Hey, so you know how you told me I shouldn't go see Dottie Howell?"

Percy gave me a wary look. "Yeah?"

"Well, I went to see her."

"Minerva!"

"It was fine, I didn't upset her." *Much.* "We had a nice visit." *Mostly.*

"I hope you didn't tell her about Keith. That's not your place."

I swatted his shoulder for having so little faith in me. "Of course I didn't. Anyway she doesn't even know there was a Keith. She thinks she's about, oh, twentyish, if I had to guess. Torn between whether to marry Del Howell or Winston Digby."

Percy made a low noise in his throat. "That's sad. But maybe not, if it spares her the pain of hearing her son is dead."

"Or of raising him."

"So did you find out anything from her?"

"A few things, actually. The Howells definitely think they're related to the Tudors, and they thought the knife belonged to Henry VIII." I started to bite my thumbnail, then realized what I was doing and snatched my hand away, clasping it with the other in my lap. "And also something else, but you're not going to like it."

"Okay."

"You heard me say Winston Digby, right? That's Ron's father. He, Dottie, and Del apparently had a little love triangle going."

"Huh, I never heard that."

"No, you didn't, and that's part of my point. Brooke's been keeping things from you."

Percy laughed. "Things like who her grandfather dated before he married her grandmother? Why would she even know that?"

I took a deep breath. "Because Dottie would have told her, if nothing else. Brooke went to see her. Dottie told me she was there. And she was asking about the knife."

"So?"

"So?"

"You were asking about the knife. Doesn't mean you did anything wrong."

I snorted. "At least I walked through the front door. They have security and stuff there, you can't just walk up to somebody's room. And they told me Dottie hadn't had any visitors. Which means Brooke had to have snuck in. Like, a full-on caper."

Percy rolled his eyes. "Something gets stolen in a caper. Are you saying Brooke robbed Dottie Howell?"

"No, fine, that's the wrong word. But she had to have used stealth and subterfuge, and if she were on the up and up, why wouldn't she just sign in, same as I did?"

"On the up and up?" Percy stopped drumming against the steering wheel and gripped it instead. "What are you suggesting, exactly? That she came home to steal the knife? That she killed Keith Howell?" His tone made it clear that both notions were absurd.

"All I'm saying is, that's noteworthy behavior. Noteworthy and suspicious."

By then we were in my apartment building's parking

lot. Percy slammed the Jeep into park and turned toward me. "Noteworthy? *Noteworthy*?" He shook his head and went on before I had a chance to answer. Not that he'd really asked a question. "By noteworthy, you mean worth noting."

"Yes, that's what the word means."

"Yeah well, I've been on the wrong end of your notes before." He jabbed a finger at me. "You are not going to tell Ruby about this, Minerva."

I had no intention whatsoever of telling Ruby anything. Not yet, anyway, not until I had some notion of what Brooke was up to. What would I even tell her? That Brooke had gone to visit the same woman I'd gone to visit, and asked her some of the same questions I had? I could just imagine how that conversation would go.

But Percy's tone left me less than inspired to say all of that. I was about to pull out the old *You are not the boss of me*, but then I remembered that he was, in fact, the boss of me. "Or what?" I crossed my arms. "You'll fire me?"

"I'll ..." He sputtered for a second. "Be really mad at you! And I'll never invite you for dinner again, which means you'll never get Dante's pie again. Is that what you want?"

No, it is not. Among other things, that pie had been very good.

Nevertheless, I felt that what I was about to say needed to be said. "The day we went to the animal shelter, I was teasing you about Brooke. And I said you couldn't be objective where she's concerned. Well, I'm not teasing now. You really can't."

"That's not fair."

"How isn't it fair?"

"You're holding the fact that I know her against me."

"That's ... kind of what *not objective* means."

"No, it's ..." Percy ran a hand through his hair, which made it stand straight up. I did not think about how adorable it looked. Certainly not while we, who were only friends, were fighting about another woman, with whom he might be more.

"If somebody told me you were acting suspiciously," he said, "I would tell them the same thing I'm telling you now—that you're incapable of killing anybody. Because I know you, right? And I know Brooke. That's not me being deluded, or manipulated, or blind. It's just me telling the truth."

"I'm not saying she killed anybody." *Not necessarily.* I cleared my throat. "But you have to admit it's weird."

"You don't even know for sure that she was there. All you have to go on is Dottie. Who is, you know ... dotty."

"Ha, ha." I pursed my lips at him.

"For all you know, Dottie's the manipulative one, and she's trying to frame Brooke, because Brooke's a Digby."

"She didn't mention Brooke by name," I said, then immediately regretted giving him a piece of ammunition like that. He gestured widely, kind of everywhere at once, I guessed to demonstrate exactly how stupid I sounded.

"But she described her," I hastened to add. "Including the scar. She wasn't out to get a Digby. She was just telling me about another woman who'd come to ask about the knife."

Percy shrugged one shoulder. "Lots of people have scars."

"Percy. It wasn't just the scar. Like I said, Dottie described the woman. It was Brooke."

"Because you've known Brooke so long you'd recognize her, among umpteen billion people in the world, just by a few words from a confused old woman?" He shook his head. "Think about this rationally."

"I'm pretty sure I'm not the one being irrational here."

He ignored that, which was probably for the best. "What reason would Brooke have to ask about the knife? What reason would she have to sneak into a home to visit Dot? What reason could she possibly have to kill Keith Howell?"

Those were the questions, weren't they? But since I didn't have any answers yet, I offered none.

Percy gave me a hard look. "You just don't like her."

"I don't even know her."

"But you're ..." He lifted his chin. "You're jealous."

"Of what, exactly?"

We stared at each other for a few seconds. My heart sped up, and I struggled not to show it on my face.

He looked away first. But he didn't answer the question.

Plant, upset that we were clearly fighting (and that we'd been sitting in the car so long) stuck his head into the front, right into Percy's face, blocking it from my view. I saw his fingers, though, curling around Plant's head to scratch it.

Such nice hands.

"Plant, get back." I gave him a shove. "We're going in."

"To do what?" Percy asked. "Not to call Ruby."

"At this hour? What, I'm going to call her at home?"

"You're not going to call her at all."

I scoffed. "And here we go. Do you really never get tired of being this bossy?"

Percy tilted his head back and heaved the sigh of the sorely put-upon. "I get tired of you and Elaine and your *you're so bossy* nonsense, I can tell you that. It's not fair. It's not like I'm this controlling guy who orders people around for fun. I only butt in when—"

"When it's to protect somebody." I studied him for a few seconds, surprised I hadn't put this all together before. I knew he was bossy, of course—that was hard to miss—and I knew how much he loved to cast himself as the white knight. But I'd never realized those were the same thing. "It's your way of riding to the rescue, as it were."

"Well then, so what?" He tossed a hand. "What's wrong with wanting to protect the people you care about?"

"Nothing. As long as it comes from a healthy place."

"What unhealthy place could concern for your friends possibly come from?"

I raised a brow at him. "Do you really want me to answer that?" *You who a few hours ago couldn't even admit your father was abusive?*

He set his jaw. "You know what, yes, I really do. I am dying to hear your expert analysis."

His goading worked. Maybe I shouldn't have let it,

but I did. "All right, fine. You know what I think? I think you were the youngest, and therefore for some length of time before you got that fancy home gym, the smallest. I think you couldn't protect your mother, or your sisters, or Tristan. And I think now you've got an almost pathological need to protect everybody—just to prove you can."

He flinched, like I'd smacked him, but he recovered almost instantly. "Cool, so we're doing that? Should we do you next? Because here's what *I* think. I think *you've* got a pathological need to find criminals behind every bush, to atone for the fact that you were too lousy a judge of character to see the actual criminal coming until she put two bullets in you."

I did not flinch. Words like *lousy* seemed uncalled for, but on the whole, it was a pretty accurate evaluation. "Fair," I said simply. "But that doesn't change the fact that Brooke demonstrably lied."

He crossed his arms. "I'm serious, Minerva. If you call Ruby to feed her some story about Brooke being a suspect, you and me are done."

What you and me? Done with what?

I almost said it out loud.

Instead I just said, "I see," before getting out of the car, opening the back, and getting Plant out too. Then I slammed the door and walked into my building without so much as a backward glance at Percy Baird.

One trait he'd left out of his analysis, possibly because he hadn't had occasion to discover it yet: I was not fond of ultimatums.

Chapter Fifteen

MY FIGHT with Percy had left me stranded. My apartment was miles from Tybryd—which meant it was miles from my car. Maybe not a lot of miles, Bryd Hollow being what it was. But too many to walk.

Sajani would never accept Plant in her car. She loved him, but she loved having dog hair and drool spots all over her seats somewhat less. That left Carrie, even though it would mean her immediately repeating the story of *why* I needed a ride to her gossip of a husband.

I texted her while I was taking Plant for his final walk of the night. *Any chance you could give me a ride in tomorrow?*

Sure, but I'm meeting Paul after work.

Don't need a ride home, car's at Tybryd.

Why? Did it break down?

And here we went. *No, Percy drove me home.*

Is that so? After ...

I rolled my eyes, then since she couldn't see that,

added an eyeroll emoji. *After DINNER. Was at his house to talk to Elaine about her wedding. But we had a fight.*

You and Elaine?

Me and Percy.

My phone rang. I tugged Plant away from the single blade of grass he'd spent the past three minutes sniffing, and answered as we started walking again.

"People leave too much out when they text," Carrie said. "What did you guys fight about?"

"Brooke Digby."

She gasped. "Because he's with her again?"

"No. I mean, maybe he is, I don't know. But the fight was more because I sort of maybe just a tiny bit accused her of murdering Keith Howell." I summarized the day's events, starting with Dottie and ending with me flouncing away from Percy's car.

"Well," Carrie said when I finished, "I don't blame you for not taking Percy's word for it when it comes to Brooke. Lovesick as he was back in the day, I'm sure she can still do no wrong in his eyes. But I know her too, and I'm with him on this one. I'll bet she was just curious, same as you are. And maybe visiting Dottie to be nice."

"Then why do it in secret?"

"You don't even know for sure that it *was* secret. Maybe the lady you talked to, who said that Dottie hadn't had any visitors, was out sick that day."

I told her she had a point, even though I didn't really think she did. There were too many other weird things about Brooke's behavior—her not wanting me to see Dottie, her lying about the cause of the family feud—for me to believe the visit had been innocent. By the time I went to bed that night, I'd resolved to find out the truth of the matter.

The trick would be to investigate Brooke Digby without appearing to investigate Brooke Digby. At least as far as Percy could see.

I called Lia at Starlight as soon as I got to the office the next morning, and left a voicemail asking her to call me back. She had no reason to give me information about the visitor logs. She probably wasn't even supposed to. But we'd gotten along well enough; I figured it was at least worth a try.

Maybe she would prove me wrong, and everybody else right, and that would be the end of it. It wasn't like I *wanted* Percy's girlfriend to be a stabby psycho.

Percy himself came stalking into the events office almost an hour after I got in. "Where were you?"

He asked the question loudly enough to disturb Sajani, who was on a call. She gave me a panicked look and fled the office, still talking on her phone. Plant, meanwhile, had started bounding toward Percy with his usual exuberance, but his ears went back and he slowed to a walk.

"It's fine, you're fine." Percy scratched Plant's head. But apparently the judgment of *fine* did not extend to me; his eyes were blazing when they met mine. "I banged on your door for like five minutes before I got the clue that Plant wasn't barking, and you must have come in without me."

Oops. Nice work, Min.

I didn't really need my inner critic to berate me;

Percy looked plenty up to the job. "I'm sorry," I said. "I got a ride with Carrie."

"And you didn't think to, oh I don't know, text me and tell me that? I am kind of a busy guy, you know."

"I'm sorry. I'm a nitwit. I should have texted, that was thoughtless. I just assumed, with you being so mad at me, that I should find my own way in." *Especially since you didn't text, either.*

"Since when have I been that much of a jerk?" Percy huffed and dropped a cardboard cup on my desk. "Here. I got you some tea. I'm sure it's cold by now."

Odsbodikins, the man had brought me tea. Was it a peace offering? "I'm sorry."

"You seem to be sorry a lot."

My lip jerked into a smile, involuntarily. It was an inside joke with us, something I'd said to him when we met.

But there was no trace of his usual humor in his face now. His expression was downright mutinous as he said, "I'm having dinner with Brooke tonight. At her family's restaurant."

What did he expect me to say to that? Was he trying to bait me into another fight? Or to get me to be unreasonable, so he could stay mad? So much for peace offerings.

Or was he trying to make me jealous? Just to prove his stupid theory that I was.

Well, he could just forget about any of that. "Give her my best." I turned back to my desk and resumed my seat. "And thanks for the tea."

I had no idea how he reacted to that, because I very steadfastly did not look at him as he left.

Plant whined and dropped onto my feet, disappointed that Percy's visit had been so short. "You and me both, buddy," I whispered. "But we might have to get used to not seeing him so much anymore."

Lia called me not long after Percy left. "So this is a weird question," I said when we'd done the usual round of greetings, "but I was wondering how sure you were, when you said that Dottie hadn't had any other visitors since you started."

"Pretty sure," she said—but she sounded hesitant. *Odsbodikins.*

But no, I reminded myself, in this particular case, it would be a good thing for me to be wrong. I could go back to suspecting Alan, for whom absolutely nobody was lovesick, probably not even his wife, and whom nobody would get mad at me for accusing.

"Hang on," Lia said, "I'm standing right at the desk, I can check the log. Let me just search for Dottie's name here ..." I heard the click of a keyboard.

"You won't get in trouble for that?"

"I wouldn't be allowed to tell you *who* came, but I don't see any harm in saying *whether* anyone did. Why do you want to know?"

"It's going to sound crazy, but I have a friend who says she was there, and I think she was lying. Maybe she just felt guilty for not visiting Dottie in so long."

Lia laughed. "So you want to make her feel even guiltier by catching her in the lie? Great friend you are."

Great friend, indeed. Especially considering I was the

one lying now. But it seemed wiser to present a petty squabble, versus suggesting somebody had eluded their security and snuck in to see Dottie, possibly for nefarious reasons, right under their collective nose.

"Nope, no visitors," Lia said a second later.

"Thank you, Lia. You've been a huge help."

That wasn't strictly true. Sure, the confirmation that Brooke was lying was *useful* information. But *helpful*, in the general context of my life (and the more specific context of Percy), it was not.

Sajani came bustling in just before lunch. She looked up at me as she bent to greet Plant, brows raised. "I don't suppose you want to tell me what that thing with Percy was about?"

"You suppose correctly. Where did you go?"

"Tour of the little inn." She tossed Plant a treat from the jar on her desk, then sat down. "Lovely old couple, scouting spots for their golden anniversary."

"Lucky you." I envied her getting to deal with nice people, while I got the likes of Bonnie Digby, who'd ended up compromising on a Thursday date in May for her wedding. But I supposed avoiding Digbys was one of the perks of seniority.

Bonnie Digby! Isn't that today?

I pulled up my calendar, then smiled to myself. I was seeing her and Bo that very afternoon. Maybe I could find a way to pump her for information about Brooke—and verify (or debunk) Brooke's alibi for the day of Keith's murder.

"What are you looking so smug about?" Sajani asked.

"Devious plotting," I said. Truthfully, as it happened.

153

"Ah"—she waved a hand—"the usual, then. I was thinking we'd leave around six tonight. That should get us there in plenty of time."

I blinked at her. "There where?"

"Rapunzel's, of course. The tasting?"

Drat. "That's tonight?"

Sajani gaped at me. "You forgot?"

"I'm sorry. I did. Nothing to worry about, though." I forced myself to smile. "I'll just have to run Plant home first, so I'll leave here a couple minutes early and meet you there."

There. As in, the same restaurant where Percy was having dinner with Brooke. Possibly at the same time.

Double drat.

Was that why he'd told me—or warned me—that he would be at Rapunzel's tonight? Had he somehow remembered that Sajani and I had the tasting, even though I myself had forgotten?

That seemed awfully unlikely, but I fervently hoped for it just the same. Otherwise, it would be more than a little awkward, me showing up during his date.

Or whatever it was. Sure, I'd had this reservation for a while, but he might not know that. He might think I was there to spy on him and Brooke. Either because I suspected Brooke, or because I was jealous of her. Or both.

I was definitely going to look like a stalker.

Which, I kind of was. But that didn't mean I wanted Percy to know that.

Chapter Sixteen

CLUES ARE SUPPOSED to make things clearer. That's basically their entire job. But what I found out that afternoon added more to my confusion than it subtracted.

I'd just finished drinking the sad, cold tea Percy had brought me, and tossing the cup into the recycle bin maybe a tiny bit more energetically than the task required, when Bonnie and Bo showed up. Ten minutes late, which was, in my brief experience with Bonnie, actually pretty punctual for her. I hadn't met Bo yet, but I'd seen him on TV. He was handsome, if you liked the cocky, overly tattooed type.

I didn't get much chance to look him over, or even introduce myself, because Bonnie let out a shriek almost as soon as they came in. Plant, in his never-ending quest to make people who disliked dogs like them even less, was heading toward her in all his wiggling glory, and this time I'd failed to catch his collar.

"Plant!" I snapped. "Sit!"

Ninety-eight percent of the time, Plant was a Very

Good Boy when he came to the office. Unfortunately for me, the two percent was generally when I most needed him to behave. He chose that moment to ignore me. He'd caught sight of something bright, and was not to be diverted from it: fabric samples poking out of the top of Bonnie's purse, no doubt to be returned.

Sensing that Bonnie wasn't sufficiently impressed with his greeting, Plant tried to snatch the fabric. Bonnie yanked her purse back to keep it from him, and dropped it instead, spilling its contents onto the floor.

"Plant!" He knew that voice, and finally did as he was told, but sitting wasn't going to be enough to get us out of this. "Get in your place!"

He slunk over to his rug, looking thoroughly disappointed in me, and turned his back on all of us as he flopped down. Bo glowered at me. Behind him, Sajani was trying very hard not to laugh.

"I'm so sorry." I got down on my knees to help Bonnie pick up her things.

With a grunt that I assumed was meant to indicate her rejection of my apology, she snatched her lipstick from my hand.

As the two of us got back to our feet, the light caught a pendant around her neck: a gold *B* on a chain of glass beads, with three of the same beads dangling from the bottom of the letter. I stared at it. Probably for long enough to be rude. Hopefully she didn't think I was staring at her chest.

But I wasn't thinking about manners, or how awkward things might look (or about Bonnie Digby's chest). I was thinking about that necklace.

I remembered seeing the chain before, dropping down under her collar. But it was the season for high-necked sweaters, and the chain was all I'd seen. Today she had on a crisp white button-down shirt, open enough to display the whole necklace.

B for Bonnie, that was obvious. For Bonnie and Brooke, and now Bonnie was marrying Bo Blue. She was going to be Bonnie Blue, wife of Bo, a thought that temporarily distracted me and almost made me laugh out loud.

The Digbys clearly had a thing for the letter *B*. It had never occurred to me to wonder why.

I smiled sweetly at Bonnie, who still looked irritated. "That necklace is beautiful. Can I ask where you got it?"

That softened her up a little. "Oh!" She touched it. "It was a gift from my father for my sixteenth birthday. Brooke has one too, but she hardly ever wears hers."

"Was it your father's idea, to name you both *B* names?"

"Yeah, I guess. I don't think my mom cared much what we were called. We're leaving the dog here, right?"

"Right. I've got some cakes set up for you in one of the conference rooms."

I led them out of the office—leaving Plant behind with Sajani—and resolved to get through the cake tasting as quickly as possible.

Bo struck me as an arrogant ratbag, not to put too fine a point on it, but at least he was efficient. It only took them half an hour to settle on the red velvet, as I knew they would, as everybody always did. The only downside was, what little conversation we had yielded no opening to talk about Brooke's whereabouts the day of the murder.

I couldn't say goodbye fast enough. As soon as they were gone, I closed myself into the now empty conference room and scrolled through my phone for a few minutes.

Then I called Ruby. "So Anne Boleyn had this necklace."

"Anne who?"

"Boleyn. You've never heard of Anne Boleyn? She was Henry VIII's second wife."

"The one he loved so much he broke up with the Pope over her?"

"Well, it's more complicated than that, but yeah." With an effort, I pressed on without lecturing her about it. "She had a necklace, it's famous, she wore it in a portrait. A strand of pearls with a *B* and three little pearls hanging down. I can text you a picture."

"Does it matter?"

"Maybe. Bonnie Digby has a pendant that looks like it."

"You're not suggesting it's the actual necklace?"

"No, no, of course not." I laughed, as if the very suggestion that I would ever be ridiculous was ridiculous. Ruby already thought I was ridiculous half the time, and it would not do to have that foremost in her mind right now. "It's not even the same. Anne's was pearls, and Bonnie's is glass beads."

"So you called to tell me that a woman owns a necklace with her first initial on it. You know, the way millions of women do?"

"I mean." I huffed. "Kind of, but it sounds stupid when you put it like that."

"And you're saying it's not stupid."

"What it is is a pretty crazy coincidence, after our conversation yesterday. Because I've been wracking my brain trying to remember where I'd seen the name of that song before, the one on the knife, and I just couldn't put my finger on it. But seeing this necklace today reminded me."

Now Ruby sounded a little more interested. "Okay, so where have you seen it?"

"It was in Anne Boleyn's song book."

"Her what?"

"She had this song book, and the knife song was in it. I just looked it up. I can send you a link."

"Okay. But lots of people probably knew the song, at the time, right?"

"Right, but only six people were married to Henry VIII."

"And that matters why?"

"The Howells think they're related to him. And that the notation knife was his. Dottie told me."

"You saw Dottie?" Ruby sounded surprised.

Oops. Would Percy be mad, that I'd told her that much?

Did I care if he was mad?

I decided to leave Brooke out of it, at least until I worked out the answer to that last question. "Yeah, I was just curious about the knife. And she said their family legend was that the knife belonged to Henry himself."

"And do you believe this?" Ruby asked. "About them

being related, obviously, not about where their knock-off knife came from."

"Well, she also told me that Henry VIII had nine wives and chopped all their heads off, so her history isn't all that reliable. But I believe that the Howells believe it, and that might be all that's relevant to the case."

"Oh, I doubt any of this is relevant to the case. I've just been humoring you out of habit."

"But it's got to mean something," I said. "It's not a coincidence that I was looking at that necklace right when you were looking into that song. Both of us, right here in Bryd Hollow."

"I think you'd be surprised by how many things people ascribe meaning to, that have no meaning at all."

"This isn't one of those things."

I could practically feel Ruby staring me down from over the top of her glasses. "Are you suggesting we're being guided by divine hand? Because I'm fairly certain the almighty has better things to do."

"No, I'm suggesting that this is an awful lot of connections to sixteenth-century England, for a small town in North Carolina. It's not unreasonable to consider whether those connections are connected to one another."

"All right, Miss Investigator, dazzle me with your wit. How are they connected?"

Sadly, I had no idea.

Ruby didn't seem to have many thoughts on the matter, either. But maybe the Digbys would, and I was eating at their restaurant that very night. Maybe I could squeeze some information out of them.

Without them realizing, of course. And more importantly, without Percy realizing.

I went back to my office to find that Sajani had stepped out, and that Plant was in dire need of consolation after being not only banished to his rug, but then left alone *without a bone*. I got down on the floor to rub his belly. "It's not you, it's Bonnie," I assured him. "She just doesn't like dogs. Probably scared of them."

I bent forward to whisper in his ear. Despite his lack of knowledge of the English language, Plant loved to feel he was being told a secret. "It would be awfully nice, though, if you would learn to mind me, and back off when I tell you to."

Plant thumped his tail, but I wasn't paying attention to him anymore. From that angle, so close to the floor, I saw that a few of the things from Bonnie's purse were still under my desk. Muttering to myself, I reached out to grab them before Plant noticed (and therefore ate) them.

A tube of mascara and two crumpled receipts. One of the latter was from the Seven Ravens in town. The other was from a coffee shop called Jaffrey Java, which I assumed, since the town of Jaffrey was half an hour away, was there.

The Jaffrey Java one was dated February sixteenth—the same day Bonnie and Brooke had come to see me.

The same day Keith Howell had died.

One caramel mocha. One vanilla latte. The timestamp read *3:52 PM*, around an hour before our meeting.

So Brooke had been in Jaffrey with her sister at four that day. Did the timing clear her of Keith's murder?

Not in itself. But though I didn't drink coffee myself, I was told the Seven Ravens made an excellent cup of it; there was no reason to drive all the way to Jaffrey just for a latte. The Digby sisters must have been doing at least some of their shopping in the vicinity of Jaffrey Java.

I vaguely remembered Brooke mentioning a dress shop. Was there one in Jaffrey? Or some other wedding-related business, where they might have spent some time —long enough to give Brooke an alibi (or not)?

I didn't know. But I meant to find out.

Chapter Seventeen

Before I could conduct any sort of investigation in Jaffrey, I had to run the gauntlet of dinner at Rapunzel's. And that turned out to be no small feat.

When Sajani and I walked in, Percy and Brooke were already sitting at a cozy table by the window, overlooking Honor Avenue and all the quaintness that was Bryd Hollow. Percy had his back to the door, so Brooke saw us first. And she did not look happy about it. The look she gave me was downright chilly.

We'd gotten along fine when we first met, but it seemed our relationship had soured. Had Percy told her anything (or, heaven forbid, everything) about our fight?

She leaned across the table and grabbed Percy's hand, laughing at something he said. Her eyes shot back to me.

It was all I could do not to roll my eyes in reply. Apparently the Percy nostalgia had taken her back so far, she'd mistaken us all for middle schoolers.

Percy must have noticed her looking over his shoulder, because he turned around. He didn't look all that happy to see me either. Although his face was more surprised than cold. Okay then, he hadn't known Sajani and I had this appointment.

I now officially looked like a stalker.

I wondered which of them he thought I was stalking: Brooke, or him.

It didn't help that, as important guests ourselves, Sajani and I were also led to a table by the window—the next one over from theirs.

There was no point in pretending we didn't know each other. Or that this wasn't awkward as all blazes. Grabbing Sajani's elbow to drag her with me, I stepped over to their table and gave them a bright, "Hey guys!"

Percy stood to greet us, but his voice was considerably less bright. "What brings you here?"

"We have a tasting tonight," Sajani said.

"It's been on our calendar for a *long time*," I added.

"Right," said Brooke, "I remember you saying it was coming up."

Which should have been good of her, but there was something condescending in her tone that I didn't like. Like she was supporting my excuse as an act of pity, but didn't actually believe it.

A server came along with the bottle of wine that Percy had apparently ordered, and I moved aside. "Well. Enjoy your dinner."

Sadly, the tables weren't close enough together to eavesdrop. Sajani sat with her back to Percy, leaving Brooke and I facing one another across both tables. With Percy's and Sajani's heads in the way, I didn't get a glimpse of Brooke often, but every time I did, she was giving Percy a dazzling smile. She kept grabbing his hand.

Twice, I caught her looking at me. And whether accurately or not, I thought I felt her eyes several more times.

Bo had prepared a special menu just for us, so I was freed from the distraction of deciding what to eat. I tried to focus on the food (which was amazing) instead of on Brooke's trilling laugh. But that laugh just did not quit. I could hardly take two bites without hearing it.

Come on, Brooke. Percy thinks *he's that funny, but we both know he's really not.*

"Minerva!" Sajani gave me an irritated look. "Have you been listening to a thing I've said?"

"No," I admitted. "Sorry. I was, um ... wool-gathering."

She raised her brows before taking a pointed look over her shoulder. Then she leaned forward, voice low, and asked, "Do you think they're back together? Paul Kwon told me they dated in high school."

Of course he did. Sajani, like me, was not a Bryd Hollow native, but Paul was always all too happy to bring people into the town gossip fold.

"I have no idea," I said. "Nor do I care."

Sajani snorted. "If you didn't care, you would've been listening to me instead of staring at them."

"I am not staring!"

"If you say so. Give me a bite of that shrimp, and try this pork belly."

Bo came out between the third and fourth courses to say hello to us, although he wasn't especially personable about it. His smiles over the compliments to his food looked a little bored, as if he considered the praise his due.

Ron Digby was much more charming when he came by before dessert, which was in keeping with my experience of him; other than that day on his porch, he was always dapperly dressed and as affable as could be. "Ladies, how's everything been?"

"Wonderful," I said.

"You've outdone yourself." Sajani gave him a wide smile. "DJ is going to be so jealous."

"You should have brought him," said Ron. "We'd have been happy to have him."

"Couldn't get a sitter."

"Next time, then. Anyway, you mean Bo outdid himself. I can't take any credit."

"No, I meant you." Sajani took a sip of wine before setting her glass down. "Rapunzel's has always been fantastic, but you've taken your game to a whole new level, snagging him."

"Glad to hear it." Ron leaned forward and stage-whispered, "He didn't come cheap."

He wasn't wearing a tie bar or pin (an odd oversight, in a restaurant) and his pale pink tie fell forward as he spoke. It was only a second before he put his palm to his chest to hold the tie back, but I thought I caught a glimpse of something, just at the bottom of the tail ...

A tiny black hair. A cat hair, maybe?

I hadn't gotten a real look at it. It could've been an eyelash, or a piece of lint. It could've been nothing more than my imagination.

But it was possible. When there was a cat—or two—in the house, even a man as well put together as Ron Digby couldn't avoid cat hair entirely.

I'd seen a white cat in the window that day. But lots of cat people had more than one cat. I'd never noticed a black hair on Bonnie or Brooke, but I'd never gotten such an up-close look at their clothes as I'd just gotten at Ron's tie. Not until today anyway, when I was on the office floor with Bonnie, and I was too distracted by her necklace at the time.

If the Digbys had a black cat, there went the one clue that didn't fit Brooke.

Though to be fair, a stray pet hair in a room that wasn't even the scene of the crime was a flimsy clue at best, whichever direction it pointed. This was probably nothing, and even if it was something, it wasn't the time or place for getting lost in thought.

I cast about for a reply to Ron's joke. "Maybe Bo will give you a better deal when he's part of the family. I just saw him and Bonnie today for a cake tasting."

"How'd that go?"

"Red velvet."

Ron shrugged. "Of course."

"Oh, and I meant to ask you," I said, as casually as I could, "not related, but speaking of Bonnie ... she was wearing a necklace today, with a *B* pendant?"

Ron looked confused, and I could hardly blame him. It had been an awkward segue, but it was the best I could do. "Yes?" he asked.

"She said you'd given it to her, and I was just

wondering if you remembered where you got it. It was so well done. I'd like to get one for my mother."

Ron's lips flattened. "I'm sorry, I don't remember. Ladies, enjoy your desserts."

He departed abruptly. Because he was busy, I wondered, or because my question had somehow upset or offended him? More food for thought—but later. Right now it would probably be good if I could listen to at least a few of the words my dining companion (and boss) was saying.

"I'm sorry, can you repeat that last thing?" I asked. "I was distracted again."

Sajani snickered. "By what, I wonder? Not the couple behind me?"

I narrowed my eyes at her. I preferred not to dwell on whether I was irritated because I didn't like the teasing, or because I didn't like the word *couple*. "So you were saying?"

"I was saying, speaking of childcare problems, can you go to the BHSBA meeting next week? It's Wednesday at three, and it doesn't usually run past five, because Ron doesn't like to miss dinner service. We haven't been to one yet this year, and this is the last one of the quarter. But DJ will be out of town and I wanted to get home early for Bina's taekwondo tournament."

"Sure, I can go." As every business in Bryd Hollow was by definition small, most of their owners were members of the Bryd Hollow Small Business Association. I knew Sajani tried to get to one of their meetings every quarter, to talk about our event needs, but I hadn't been to one yet.

This one seemed like it might be good timing. Ron Digby was the president of the BHSBA, and the meetings were held in a back room here at Rapunzel's. Keith Howell had been a member, as well. Maybe this would be a good opportunity for me to reacquaint myself with just how many people in town hadn't liked the man. Maybe I'd find some less inconvenient suspects to consider.

But for now, convenient or not, I pretty much just had the one.

Rapunzel's had been redecorated after they hired Bo, to refresh the whole place, which was handy for me. Before we left, I took a few pictures of the interior with my phone. For our files, I said. To show prospective clients, I said. And those things were true.

But Percy and Brooke were still at their table, lingering over coffee. (Percy didn't even like coffee that much. He always had tea with me.)

I made sure I got Brooke in one of the photos.

Digby.

It was right there, on the chart, for all the heavens to witness. Around the turn of the seventeenth century, a new branch grew from the Boleyn family tree, via Anne's sister Mary and down through several generations of Knollyses: Digby.

Were these Digbys related to the Bryd Hollow Digbys? I didn't know; it would take a great deal more research, possibly through records I didn't have access to, to find out. But judging from those knock-off Boleyn necklaces, Ron Digby thought so. Which probably meant Brooke Digby thought so, too.

I reached over and scratched Plant's ear. "Tudors and Boleyns, Plant."

Plant heaved a sigh, got up, turned his back on me, and flopped back down on the bed. It was bad enough I'd gone out for dinner and brought him back nothing. Now I had the light on *past eleven o'clock*. Anybody who tells you dogs can't tell time doesn't really know any dogs.

"Fine." I closed my laptop and turned off the light, snuggling under my covers. But even if Plant was done with the whole topic of Tudors and Boleyns, I was not.

"In the same small, North Carolina town," I murmured. "What are the chances?"

Well, pretty low, of course. Maybe even zero. But the idea had clearly struck the fancies of the families in question. And now it had struck mine.

I thought of Anne Boleyn, whose life could have been saved by the birth of a healthy son. Instead she'd given birth to a daughter who would take the throne and usher in a golden age.

And I thought of Molly Towe—originally a Digby— who'd cursed the Howells to have only sons, never daughters. As if to say, *All right then, Tudor. You want sons? I'll give you sons.*

Like I said, fanciful. The word *absurd* wouldn't have been entirely misplaced.

But one thing was definitely true: small-town grudges ran *deep*.

Chapter Eighteen

I STOOD on the sidewalk outside Jaffrey Java, looking up and down the generic strip mall it stood in. My first thought was how lucky I was to live in a town with character. My second was about how the Bairds had founded that town, and how one Baird in particular was going to be furious with me.

Especially if tracing Brooke's whereabouts on February sixteenth revealed that she'd had time to kill Keith Howell.

If she was guilty, Percy would hate me, which I would obviously not enjoy. If she was innocent, she might ride off into the sunset with Percy, and I wasn't sure how I would feel about that. Or at least, that was what I was still telling myself at the time.

I'd already been to Jaffrey's sole formalwear shop, a frankly dingy place that I could not see Bonnie deigning to patronize. Her awful taste didn't come cheap. My inkling that the Digby sisters hadn't been there supported by two saleswomen shaking their heads when I showed them the picture of Brooke I'd taken the night before.

And that was pretty much it for Jaffrey, as far as the wedding business was concerned. Tybryd weddings were largely a package deal; there wasn't a lot for the bride to shop for apart from clothes and music. (Or in the case of this particular bride, livestock.) It was possible they'd been seeing a musician privately. Or a specialty vendor, like Keith Howell had been.

But there was another, stronger possibility. The strip mall that housed Jaffrey Java wasn't on a major road. There was nothing else in close walking distance. Which meant that whatever they'd been doing when they decided to grab a coffee, it was probably in one of the other stores there.

Hence my standing there, staring at signs and trying not to feel that this whole mission was a no-win situation.

A Mexican restaurant. A dry cleaner. A martial arts studio. These all seemed unlikely. That covered everything to the right of Jaffrey Java. To its left were a deli, a drug store, a gift card shop, and a place called Something Old Something New.

I walked over to the latter and checked out the window display: a rolling desk, a Victorian doll, a mannequin in a vintage dress. Lots of something olds, no something new in sight. Bryd Hollow had an antiques shop of its own, so I supposed there was no more reason for Brooke and Bonnie to stop here than there was to stop at any of the other stores.

Unless, maybe, you wanted to ask about a particular

old thing, without people knowing you were asking about it. Brooke had secretly questioned Dottie about the knife. Had she also secretly questioned an expert?

And if so, why would she have been making these inquiries on the same day Keith was killed with, and probably over, that same knife? I imagined a scenario in which she'd lined up a buyer for it—maybe the owner of this shop, or maybe somebody he or she found for her—sometime prior to Keith's murder.

Then, as I'd posited all along, Keith had caught the thief in the act. Brooke and Keith struggled, and Keith was stabbed.

And then Brooke came here, what, at most an hour or two later, to tell the buyer the deal was off? That seemed oddly cool-headed for somebody who'd left the knife behind in Keith's skull, presumably out of panic.

But supposing the truth of it was something along those lines, would that mean that Brooke thought the notation knife was real? Or would she have been willingly trying to sell a counterfeit antiquity to some unsuspecting collector? I supposed the little tale I'd spun worked either way.

And what about Bonnie? Was she in on it too, or had she gone to get the coffee, unaware of her sister's true motivation, while Brooke popped into this shop?

Maybe somebody in Something Old Something New could shed some light on the matter for me.

I had a fleeting thought, as I walked through the door to the tinkle of an old-fashioned bell, that I really wished Plant were with me. Which was weird, because this was not the sort of place you wanted to bring a great lumbering beast with a penchant for stealing and destroying things. The aisles were narrow, and extremely cluttered. Plant would've had me bankrupt inside fifteen minutes.

But he was my security blanket, when it came down to it. A trained guard dog, though he rarely showed it, who'd been given to me at a time when I needed guarding. I always wanted him with me, when I was nervous. And for reasons I couldn't quite specify, I was nervous now.

I was not put at ease by the person behind the counter, a slender man with salt-and-pepper hair and thin lips. I couldn't see his eyes; he was wearing sunglasses, despite the relatively dimly lit shop. Mirrored sunglasses. In chunky, white plastic frames.

"Help you?" he asked.

"Um. Maybe." My plan had been to show him the picture of Brooke, just as I'd done at the formalwear shop, but I hesitated. I didn't *think* those were the sort of sunglasses a person wore for medical reasons, but what if I was wrong? Would it be rude to ask him to examine a picture?

Maybe I ought to try a different approach. "I wanted to ask about a specific antiquity. A knife, with musical notes—"

"Notation knife?" he interrupted, then laughed. "Popular subject."

"Somebody else was asking about them, too?"

"Could be."

That seemed to be all he was going to say. Was I

supposed to offer him a bribe or something? I bit my lip. "Okay. Well, I'm also looking for somebody."

"Don't sell bodies," he said. "Name of the store is Some*thing* Old Some*thing* New."

"I was just wondering if you could tell me whether she's been in here. Maybe she was the other person asking about the knife?"

"Got a picture?"

Why yes, yes I do. I took out my phone, zoomed in on Brooke's smiling (at Percy) face, and held it out to him. "She might have been with somebody, another woman."

He looked at the picture with no apparent difficulty, though he didn't lift the glasses. Maybe he was just wearing them because he was hungover, or had a migraine. Or because he was a weirdo. "Yep."

"Yep, she's been in here?" I asked. "Or yep, she was with somebody, or yep, she's the one who asked about the knife?"

"You competing with her?"

"Could be."

"All right, why not, I'll tell you the same thing I told her. I don't mind selling to more than one."

"Selling?" I blinked at him. "Selling what? Wasn't she the one doing the selling?"

The man was quiet for a moment, during which I had no idea what was going on behind his mirrored frames. "You know what?" he said finally. "It's kind of dark in here, and I have this headache today. Not sure I recognize her, after all."

Odsbodikins. What had I said wrong?

I took a twenty-dollar bill from my wallet, dropped it

by accident, picked it up off the (sticky, which was a little disconcerting) floor, and held it against the back of my phone. My subtle way of suggesting I was willing to pass him both.

Ready for a career as a hard-boiled PI, I was not. "Can I show you the picture again?"

But he shook his head. "Sorry, screen hurts my eyes. You're welcome to browse the store, but I wouldn't have any notation knives. They're very rare, you know."

"Yes. I do know."

He stepped back to lean against the wall behind the counter, and crossed his arms. "Anything else you're looking for?"

"No. Thank you for your time, Mr. ..."

"Welcome."

I assumed that was in response to the thanks, and that his name was not Mr. Welcome, although that would have been an amusing irony. With a parting nod, I walked slowly down the center aisle toward the door, glancing at a few things on my way by. Maybe if I was pokey enough, he'd change his mind about earning that twenty dollars.

My eyes fell on an antique doll, and I picked it up. He *had* told me I was welcome to browse. Gently, I turned the doll over, shifting aside her little hat to look at the maker's mark on the back of her neck.

Then frowned. The mark was interrupted by a line, where the porcelain head had been attached to the delicate porcelain neck.

I turned the doll over again and looked into her

brown glass eyes. "Can you tell me about what year this doll was made?" I called.

Mr. Welcome sauntered to the edge of the counter and leaned over it for a better look. I held up the doll.

"Early nineteenth century," he said.

"*Early* nineteenth?"

"That's what I said."

"Great." I set the doll back down. "Thanks again."

I got out of the shop as fast as I could, then stopped at Jaffrey Java to grab a cup of tea and a piece of banana bread to go, by way of calming my nerves. I ate the bread in my car, chewing slowly while I reflected on the events of the past half hour.

Searching for any way to interpret them other than the way I was.

Dating notation knives might have required an expert, but dating antique dolls did not. As it happened, my mother, and in more recent years my sister, collected them. I knew a thing or two about them.

Like for example, that glass eyes hadn't been used until the latter part of the nineteenth century. It was, of course, possible that Mr. Welcome didn't know his business as well as he should, and was simply mistaken about the year.

What wasn't possible was for a genuine antique doll's head to be attached to its neck like that. The head, neck, and shoulders would have been made from a single mold, then attached to the stuffed body, usually via holes in the shoulders.

That doll was a fake. A fake made by a not-especially-gifted counterfeiter. Just like the knife.

And Mr. Welcome had offered to sell me something. Just as by his own admission he'd offered to sell Brooke Digby something.

Except maybe he'd succeeded with her.

I might have set out to poke into Brooke's alibi, but I'd ended up poking a hornet's nest. And it looked an awful lot like Brooke Digby was the queen hornet.

Chapter Nineteen

I WAS STILL DRIVING HOME when I called Bonnie. I'd gotten way too jittery already, and I was afraid if I waited any longer than that, I'd lose my nerve.

Not that I intended to accuse Bonnie of anything. I wasn't sure about her. She'd been with Brooke in Jaffrey, but that didn't mean she'd been *with* Brooke in Jaffrey. Mr. Welcome hadn't said anything about her either way. And *she* hadn't gone to visit Dottie and lied about it. She might very well be oblivious to this whole thing.

But I was sure about her sister.

Bonnie answered right away; women were always in for their wedding planners. "Do *not* tell me there's a problem with the flowers."

"The fl—no. We don't even ... your wedding is two months away."

"What is the problem, then?" she asked.

"There is no problem. I just need your sister's phone number."

Bonnie sighed heavily. "Are you two fighting over

Percy? Because obviously I'd have to take my sister's side. Which would mean firing you. Which would be a bummer, because against all odds you've actually been doing a really good job, and—"

"We're not fighting about anything," I cut in, forcing a laugh. "She's your maid of honor. I have *things* I need to discuss with her."

"Ohhhh!" Bonnie practically squealed the word, no doubt thinking, just as I'd intended her to, that we were planning some special surprise for her. "Sure, sure, I'll text you the contact."

"Thanks. Oh, and while I have you, one other question, and don't ask me why I want to know. Do you have a black cat?"

"Mr. Snugglefluff is white," Bonnie said. "He's the only cat *I* have. Endora is black, but she's my mom's. I'll be good and not ask, but just so you know, I don't want Endora in the wedding."

"Got it."

As promised, Bonnie sent me the contact as soon as we hung up, but I didn't call Brooke yet. I waited until I was safely home, with Plant beside me on the couch. Then took the coward's way out and texted her.

Brooke, hi, this is Minerva Biggs. Do you have a minute?

As soon as I hit send (and it was therefore too late to do anything about it), I huffed at myself. *Do you have a minute?* What a stupid thing to say. I wanted way more than one.

But I guessed she didn't even have the one, because it was ten minutes before she answered. I spent the bulk of that time staring at the phone, my hands shaking a little. Plant sensed my agitation and started furiously licking the side of my face. Which didn't help, but I appreciated the effort.

Finally, through the accumulation of drool on my screen, came Brooke's answer: *Sure Min what's up.*

Min? We were not close enough to be shortening one another's names. And that period instead of a question mark, indicating that she didn't *really* want to know what was up. And probably that she was annoyed.

Well, let her be.

Need to talk to you about something, it's important. Can you meet me?

Today?

ASAP.

A three-minute delay, and then: *Now's not a good time. And tell me this is not about Percy.*

It's not about Percy! What was with these Digby girls today? Fine, she wanted to be blunt? I could be blunt. *It's about the notation knife. And Keith Howell. Doubt you want me to say more over text.*

Five more minutes before a single word came back: *Where?*

I closed my eyes, not sure whether I was disappointed or relieved or vindicated or sorry. Or just scared. The very fact that she agreed to meet after what I'd just said— because of what I'd just said— seemed to confirm the worst.

Which you would think would discourage me from inviting a suspected violent notation-knife murderer into my home. In twenty-eight years, I'd been shot by no fewer than two desperate women. Did you win a set of cookware or something, if you made it to three before thirty? I wasn't eager to find out.

But Plant was leaning against me, and his comforting presence reminded me of how much I'd missed him at Something Old Something New. He was my shield. I wanted him with me for this.

Especially since, by the time it was over, he might be the only friend I had left.

He wouldn't be welcome inside the Seven Ravens or the diner, and it was too cold outside to meet in the park. Not to mention that I didn't want us to be overheard. I might not even want us to be seen.

The story in my head still held that Keith's death was more or less an accident, the result of a nasty surprise followed by a struggle. I didn't think Brooke was likely to get violent with me. And if she tried, I was pretty confident Plant could and would protect me.

It wasn't like she had a gun; if she did, she'd have used that to kill Keith. I was safe from a gunshot wound this time.

I hoped.

I texted her my address. She replied that she'd be over in fifteen minutes. That she'd gone so easily from *not a good time* to *on my way* only further reinforced my suspicions.

What should I do? Make tea? I had some cookie dough. Were cookies an acceptable accompaniment to a demand that somebody turn herself in to the police to spare you doing it for her?

I decided on the cookies, on the grounds they

couldn't hurt, and put on a pot of water for tea. That would have to do; I didn't have a coffee maker, and I wasn't about to serve her alcohol.

By the time I finished all these preparations, Brooke Digby was knocking on my door.

Nope. Make that Percy Baird knocking on my door. With Brooke at his side.

Had I not specified that she should come alone? I was about to ask this question, all righteous indignation, when I realized I probably hadn't.

But surely that was implied. You didn't just take it upon yourself to invite Bairds over to people's apartments.

Brooke shrugged in response to my obviously confused and probably equally obviously annoyed face. "I was at his house when you texted. I showed him, and he wanted to come."

Percy himself didn't say a word. He was too busy glowering at me while he gave Plant the customary scritches. At least he wasn't taking it out on my dog.

Anyway it was his own fault he was upset. Who'd told him to come sticking himself in the middle of this? Well, Brooke, I guessed. But not me, that was the main thing. I looked away, and did not meet his eye again as I ushered them in and offered them tea and cookies.

I told myself to look on the bright side; it would hardly be putting her best foot forward for Brooke to try to kill me in front of Percy.

Unless he tried to kill me first. He sat on the couch. Brooke sat beside him. Plant immediately jumped up and wedged his way between them, half on Percy's lap.

This left me alone in the armchair. I put the pot of tea, three mugs, and a plate of cookies on the coffee table between us, then warned Plant to ignore said cookies. All those things needed to be done. It wasn't like I was stalling. Much.

But now there were no excuses left. "So," Brooke said, "what's this about?"

"Well." I bit into a cookie, trying to look unfazed and confident, but it backfired. It was like sawdust going down.

I started to choke. Percy half rose from his seat, which was nice of him considering he was probably more than half wishing that cookie would kill me, but I waved him off. I took a gulp of tea—way too hot. It seared my mouth while the cookie wreaked havoc on my throat.

All in all, by the time I spoke again, my voice sounded a little broken. "It's mostly about how I'm pretty sure you killed Keith Howell, but that in deference to my good friend Percy here, I didn't want to call Ruby about it until I gave you a chance to turn yourself in."

Percy sprang up and started yelling at me. Plant, who'd never backed away from protecting me in his life, tucked his tail and looked uncertainly between us before attaching himself to my side. His hackles were up, but instead of growling, he whimpered.

Brooke started laughing, which quieted Percy down. He looked back at her. But she was looking at me. "So you've decided I'm some sort of competition for you, and that a good way to solve that problem is to send me to jail?"

I crossed my arms. "I am really getting sick of idiotic accusations of competition and jealousy."

"I'm getting sick of idiotic accusations of murder," Brooke said with a shrug. "Does that make us even?"

"No." I transferred my glare from her to Percy. "It's presumptuous, and even if it weren't, it's incredibly offensive for you to assume I'm petty enough to act like some kind of mean girl. The only part of this that's personal is the fact that I've held off on accusing her or telling anybody else what I know *for your sake*."

"What you know?" Brooke leaned back and stretched her arms over the back of the couch, like she was settling in to watch a movie. "Great. Tell us what you think you know."

I summarized everything I knew about Brooke Digby's movements, starting with the visit to Dottie at some unknown time, and ending with her visit to Mr. Welcome on the day Keith was murdered. I rounded all of this out with the Boleyn-Digby connection, and the Howell-Tudor connection, and the connections between the knife, a king, and the queen he'd beheaded. (Well, the first queen he'd beheaded.)

"So." Percy was still fuming, although he made a point of stroking Plant's ears to soothe the poor dog. "You've decided she killed Keith Howell because she visited an old lady and dropped into an antiques store. That about the size of it?"

"No!" I tossed my hands. "It's not even really an antiques st—he's a counterf—have you listened to a word I've said?"

185

"I've listened to all of them," Percy said. "At least two out of three were completely bonkers."

I shook my head. "They make perfect sense, if you're willing to open your eyes. How about I spell it out for you."

"Oh, please do," said Brooke. Which I found interesting. Wouldn't an innocent person have gotten up and left by now? But a guilty person might stay and listen, because they might want to know just how much evidence I had, and what it was.

"All right." I leaned forward in my chair, elbows on my knees. "From the beginning, then. The Howells seem pretty proud of that knife, but as far as I can tell, its existence was a surprise to Ruby and most everybody else in town. Meaning they didn't flaunt it to anybody but friends, like Dottie. So maybe you didn't know about it until recently, and that's why you stirred all this up now. Maybe you heard a rumor, and you went to visit Dottie to confirm it."

"This is a lot of maybes for someone who claims to know so much," said Brooke.

"The maybes aren't important," I said. "The main thing is, you found out about the knife. You even saw it —you must have, because you knew the details well enough to copy it. You figured out that the song on it was from Anne's songbook. At which point you decided this priceless object rightfully belonged to the Digbys, not the Howells."

"Because of Anne Boleyn," Percy said flatly.

I shrugged. "If the knife belonged to Henry, but came to him via the wife he executed—after framing her for adultery—you can see why her descendants might think they had a claim to it."

Percy snorted. "So according to you, these two random—*American*—families have been squabbling over a piece of cutlery ever since some English king cut his wife's head off in fifteen-something?"

"1536," I provided, possibly not as helpfully as I thought. "And I don't think there's any statute of limitations on squabbles, when something that valuable is involved. People find ways to put prices on priceless things all the time. Usually high ones. But since you bring up how long it's been ..."

I cocked my head at Brooke. "You guys have clearly claimed this Boleyn connection for some time, if your father was naming his daughters with *B* names and commissioning that necklace for them. And we know the Howells have claimed their Tudor connection for some time. I wonder how long *some time* is. A few generations? Even before Molly Towe put her curse on the Howell family? Maybe that's the true source of the feud."

Brooke rolled her eyes. "Another maybe."

"And like the others, it doesn't really matter," I said. "It also doesn't matter whether the Digbys are really related to the Boleyns, or the Howells to the Tudors, or whether the notation knife is real, or whether it really belonged to either Henry VIII or Anne Boleyn."

"You know the knife isn't real," Percy interjected.

I shook my head. "I know there's *a* counterfeit knife; I don't know whether *the* knife is counterfeit." I noted his impatient expression and waved all this away. "I'll get to that in a second. The point is, every one of those things could be false, and at least some of them almost certainly are, but it doesn't matter, because the people involved thought they were true."

I looked back at Brooke. "Keith had a priceless artifact that you were pretty sure ought to be yours. He obviously wasn't going to give it to you. You didn't want to steal it outright, because things might get complicated if he noticed it was missing. So you made an arrangement with the owner of Something Old Something New, and he made you something new that looked an awful lot like something old."

"So I could swap it for the real one," Brooke kindly supplied. Except it sounded kind of ridiculous, when she said it.

"Exactly," I said. "So you broke into Keith's house to make the switch. Nobody should have gotten hurt. But he caught you. There was an argument, it escalated. Maybe he was the one who came after you first. Or maybe his cat. Either way, it ended with the fake knife in Keith's eye. It probably would've been better to take that with you, but you aren't exactly a seasoned killer. You never meant for this to happen, and the blood, and the realization of what you did, was all too much. You panicked and ran—didn't even bother to close the front door behind you."

"Yet I had the presence of mind to put the real knife in my purse first?" Brooke asked.

"I don't know where the real knife is now," I admitted. "But I think it likely you took it, yes. I don't really need to know, because that's Ruby's thing, and she's pretty good at her job. I might not have the physical evidence to back all this up, but I'm confident that it exists. For one thing, I can't imagine you can stab a guy in the eye without getting some blood on you."

Brooke smirked. "Thanks for sharing, your confidence is very entertaining."

I returned the smile, as if both it and the compliment had been genuine. "Be that as it may. You seem like a strong-willed woman, I'm sure that once you got home, you found a way to quash that panic and think fast. I'll bet you wanted to offload the knife as quickly as possible, now that it was tied to a murder. Maybe your friend the counterfeiter had already lined up a buyer for you, being a shady dealer and all, and probably knowing other shady dealers. Or maybe you just wanted to ask him to line one up. Either way, you grabbed Bonnie, because an afternoon of wedding planning would make a fizzing alibi, and you went to Something Old Something New."

Brooke did everything but slow clap. She beamed at me. She pressed her hand to her chest. She declared that I was *amazing*. "Except, we went to Something Old Something New because he had a picture of a tiara on his website that I thought we might want for Bonnie. I had no idea it was likely to be fake, by the way, so I do appreciate that."

"Are we done here?" Percy got up.

"You can be done any time you want," I snapped. "Nobody asked you to come here. But I've honored your wishes long enough, and now that I know about this counterfeiter guy ..." I drifted off and spread my hands. Honestly, I didn't understand how he could still not see, after hearing my whole spiel.

He made a disgusted noise and walked to the door. Brooke got up to follow.

"I'll give you until tomorrow to think about what you want to do," I said to her. "After that, I'm going to see Ruby."

"Knock yourself out," she said with a light laugh.

Fine, let her mock. What did I care if she used this grace period wisely? Giving it to her hadn't been part of my original plan anyway, but Percy coming with her was an unexpected insurance policy. It would look way too suspicious if I were attacked now. Besides, I had a trained guard dog. Who would apparently attack anybody who tried to hurt me, as long as it wasn't Percy.

Percy walked out without another word, or so much as a glance at me. But Brooke paused at the door and turned around, looking positively delighted. I guessed because she felt I'd just made a fool of myself in front of a guy we were fighting over. Good thing both parts of that sentence were definitely absurd.

"Hey," she said, "thanks for the cookies."

Chapter Twenty

"WHAT DO YOU MEAN, she couldn't have done it?"

I sank into the chair opposite Ruby's desk, completely flummoxed. I'd spent the past half hour explaining, in painstaking detail, all about how I was sure Brooke Digby had killed Keith Howell.

Ruby was unsympathetic to my plight. She picked up the receipt from Jaffrey Java, pushed her glasses up her nose, and looked at it one more time. "You just proved she didn't do it."

"I just ... proved she ... what?"

"Keith Howell was killed sometime around four o'clock. So unless Brooke was in two places at once—"

"But you said it was between one and five!"

"When did I say that?"

"That night, when you showed me the knife and told me to give Roark my alibi."

Ruby shrugged. "That was the medical examiner's guess at first glance, but she's narrowed it down since. More importantly, *I've* narrowed it down since. You know, I did some investigating, the way us police officers like to do from time to time."

I swallowed. "And?"

"And Keith showed up, alive if not well, at the BHSBA meeting at three. He left early, but I have witnesses that put him at Rapunzel's at around three-thirty. Then you have to add enough time to that for him to get home and get stabbed. So."

"So Brooke and Bonnie weren't even in Bryd Hollow," I said—faintly, because I felt a little faint. "Brooke couldn't have done it."

"There it is." Ruby tapped her palms against her desk. "I knew you'd get there eventually. You're not quick, but you're not stupid."

I closed my eyes and dropped my forehead into my hand. This was a disaster. Not only had I been wrong, I'd been wrong in front of people. *Percy* people.

"But what about Dottie?" I looked up at Ruby. "Why did Brooke go see her, and ask about the knife?"

"It is not a crime to visit a lonely old woman."

"And Something Old Something New," I went on. "That guy is definitely a counterfeiter. Those dolls are fake. And he knew something about the knives. He has to know something about Keith's death. It's not—"

"I'll be looking into him," Ruby interrupted. "And I do thank you for the tip. But it's not a crime to visit an antiques shop either. You don't have any evidence that Brooke even knew his things were fake."

"She must have," I insisted. "It's too many coinci-dences. She might not have done the actual stabbing, but she's involved in Keith's death somehow."

I had to be right about that. Brooke Digby had to be guilty of something.

Because if she wasn't, I was *such* a ratbag.

~

PERCY HATED ME.

At least, I assumed he did, on the basis of his total silence. There were no punny texts, no cups of tea, no invitations to walk Plant through the hedge maze. Definitely no donuts.

Sure, I could've texted *him,* and brought *him* tea, and tried to make peace. But the fact of it was, I was a coward. Assuming his hatred was a very different thing from confronting it head on. I surely didn't want to see any hatred in his face.

And besides, it wasn't like I was so thrilled with him, either. He'd taken Brooke's side without the slightest hesitation. That I might be right never even entered his head.

Of course, I wasn't right, but that was not the point. The point was, he'd chosen her (whom, okay fine, he'd known his whole life) over me (whom, okay fine, he'd known for six months). And it hadn't even been a hard decision.

I might have admired his loyalty, had I not been on the wrong side of it. But as things were, I was decidedly miffed with Percy Baird.

Bonnie called the events office to insist that Sajani handle her wedding from here on out. One of the few bright sides of the whole thing, but I wondered whom else Brooke had told.

I guessed I was about to find out, because the day after I talked to Ruby, I had to go to the BHSBA meeting —at Brooke's father's restaurant.

I got there ten minutes early, in hopes of avoiding a scene if Ron kicked me out. I didn't see Ron straight off, but my friend Gretchen was standing alone by the refreshments table. I quickly crossed the room, meeting nobody's eye, to join her.

"Boxed cookies and bad coffee," she hissed. "Again."

That struck me as odd, given we were in Bryd Hollow's best restaurant, along with the owners of two other restaurants, a pub, a coffee shop, and a bakery. There was a lot of fizzing food to be had in Bryd Hollow. It was one of my favorite things about the place.

But I had more important questions on my mind. I leaned toward Gretchen and lowered my voice. "You haven't heard any gossip or rumors about me, have you?"

"I heard you went psycho on Brooke Digby in a jealous rage over Percy. Is that what you mean?"

I did not appreciate Gretchen's matter-of-fact tone, like this had come as no surprise to her at all. "*That's* the story she's telling?" I huffed. "And you believed it?"

"No, no," Gretchen assured me. "Not the psycho part, anyway. There are always two sides, and I'm sure Brooke's side paints as nasty a picture of you as it can. But eh"—she shrugged—"the jealousy thing I could believe."

"I am not jealous, and this has nothing to do with Percy!"

It had come out too loud. People started to stare. I

cleared my throat and prepared to defend myself, but was interrupted by the trudging, muttering arrival of Alan Howell. I hadn't seen him since the funeral; Tracey had already gone home to their boys. He looked as greasy and disagreeable as ever.

I assumed he'd come for cookies rather than conversation, but he offered me a smile. Or his best approximation of a smile, which was more like a grimace. "Heard you got violent with that Digby girl."

My mouth dropped open. *"Violent?"*

"Full-on catfight, is what I heard."

"Catfight? *Really?*" I made no effort to hide my disgust. This was a bridge entirely too far. "Nothing even remotely like that happened, and I resent ..."

I drifted off, realizing something: if I understood this rumor correctly, nobody, not even Keith's own son, knew that my disagreement with Brooke had anything to do with Keith's murder.

And why would that be?

There'd only been the three of us in my apartment that day, and Percy was definitely not one to spread rumors. This was Brooke's story. Had she made it about Percy just because that made me look worse? Or did she maybe not want her name associated with the crime, even if it was to refute that association? If she were guilty (of something ... or anything) it might seem wiser to not put the idea into people's heads at all.

"Alan!" Ron Digby strode over to us, straightened out the paper cups, and turned to Alan with a smile that didn't look the least bit pained. I remembered the scene between these two at Keith's funeral, and decided Ron was either a very good actor, or in a very good mood. "What brings you here?"

Alan looked indignant, but then again it was difficult to differentiate his indignant face from his default face. "My father was a member, wasn't he?"

"Of course," said Ron. "I just didn't realize you'd be staying in town and taking over his business. Businesses."

"I won't. I intend to sell everything with the house."

"But ..." That smile of Ron's was starting to look a little puzzled now. "This is a meeting for business owners."

Alan crossed his arms. "My father ought to have been here, so I'm here in his stead to represent the interests of the Howells. It would be an abuse of your power as president to kick me out, and don't think I wouldn't let everyone know it."

"Don't be silly." Ron laughed. "You're perfectly welcome. If you'll excuse me, I'd better get us started." He nodded at Gretchen and me, his first acknowledgement of us. "Ladies."

As far as I could tell, he had no particular reaction to me at all. Which might confirm that he was indeed an excellent actor. Or it might suggest that he was one of the few people Brooke hadn't mentioned our fight to at all.

And why would *that* be?

The meeting was duly called to order, and I found a folding chair beside Gretchen to await my spot on the agenda. What followed was a good hour of petty complaints, posturing, and not-very-thinly-veiled insults among the various business owners of Bryd Hollow. Basil did not appreciate that the patrons of Cullen's sometimes parked in front of *his* store. Tim Cullen noted that the space in front of Basil's store was in fact a public street, that it wasn't up to Basil to police public parking, and furthermore it was not Tim's problem if Basil didn't have enough customers to fill the spaces himself. Meanwhile, Jory from the Seven Ravens and Tony from Deirdre's diner had some sort of dispute involving coffee beans, while Lacey from By Bread Alone felt that Jory's cupcakes were stepping on her bakery's toes.

It was interminable, honestly.

"No wonder Keith Howell left early the day he died," I whispered to Gretchen. "Maybe he had a premonition that he didn't have much time left, and didn't want to spend it like this."

I'll admit it was in poor taste, but that was how Gretchen's sense of humor was. I expected her to laugh, and she did. She leaned toward me and whispered back, "Just hope Ron sticks around long enough this time to introduce you."

What? "What?"

"The last meeting. Ron left the second he called it to order. Claimed there was an urgent issue in the kitchen, but he never came back." Gretchen nodded at the small window that faced the back parking lot. "I saw him going to his car not a minute after he left, so unless the kitchen in question was somewhere else, he was just making an excuse to sneak out."

I stared at her. "Did anybody else notice?" *And did anybody tell Ruby?*

"Not that they mentioned, but I doubt anyone really cared either way. Nobody much respects Ron's authority. The only reason he's president is that we get to have the meetings here, and sometimes he feeds us."

"You don't think anybody else could come up with some stale cookies?"

"Well, he used to feed us better than that." Gretchen shook her head sadly. "I think it cost him a fortune, getting that celebrity chef. Probably thought it would pay off by now, but he did it going right into the slow season, what did he expect?"

She went on talking, about how she hoped things would pick up in the spring, and there would once again be assorted appetizers and tea cakes for the BHSBA to enjoy, but I was only half listening.

I'd known all along that Bo Blue was expensive, but how expensive were we talking? If Ron couldn't afford to put out snacks for people he wanted to impress, it must have been quite a strain.

On top of his wife's treatments. And now his daughter's wedding. I had firsthand knowledge that she was sparing no expense.

All together, it might be enough to make a man's situation pretty desperate.

And the man in question had left the last meeting even before Keith did.

Chapter Twenty-One

So Brooke Digby was guilty after all, but she had an accomplice. Or probably it was the other way around: she was her father's accomplice.

It all made sense. Keith Howell had been complaining to Ruby about break-ins, or attempted break-ins, in the weeks leading up to his murder. If the killer had wanted to make a copy of the knife to swap for the real one, he would need a few things in advance. Pictures of the knife, for Mr. Welcome to work from. And before that, knowledge of the knife's location in Keith's house, whether it was locked up, how to access it.

Our villain would have worn gloves for that search, but gloves weren't immune to cat hair. He'd left one of Endora's hairs behind in the apothecary cabinet. Maybe he'd left a few somewhere else, too, and Keith had found those.

Maybe Keith hadn't realized it was the knife, specifically, that was in danger, but he knew somebody was up to something. And Ron Digby was one of his biggest enemies. Keith might even have spotted a scratch or bite mark on Ron, courtesy of Suffolk or Buckingham, to raise his suspicions.

And then Ron stole away from the BHSBA meeting. As soon as Keith realized he wasn't coming back, he left too, and went home.

The rest could have gone pretty much the same way I'd guessed it happened with Brooke. The interruption, the struggle. Keith ending up dead. The killer fleeing the scene.

Where did Brooke fit in? She'd done a lot of the legwork, visiting Dottie and Mr. Welcome. Maybe it was her job to find a buyer for the real knife. Maybe that was what she'd been doing at Something Old Something New that day, unaware that back in Bryd Hollow, things had just gone horribly wrong.

I remembered her face, when I told her and Bonnie there'd been violence at Keith Howell's house. She'd been shaken. Now I understood why.

Not that I could tell anybody else any of this, after my latest debacle. I definitely couldn't go accusing Ron Digby of anything until I had proof. Preferably physical proof—like the real knife.

Had they already sold it? Ron had been in an awfully good mood at the meeting. Maybe that meant the knife was gone already. Or maybe he was just happy because they'd found a buyer, and would be rid of it soon.

I needed to find out which it was, and I only knew of one person, apart from the Digbys, who might be able to tell me. The morning after the BHSBA meeting, I searched the North Carolina business registry and found Mr. Welcome's real name: Earnest Beale.

Earnest? Hadn't seen that one coming. It was even more ironic than Mr. Welcome.

As soon as my lunch break rolled around, I put Plant in the car, and went to pay Earnest a visit.

I had zero intention of using Plant to intimidate anybody. Less than zero. I'd once learned a very hard lesson, where that was concerned. My main goal was protection, which seemed like a good thing to have when confronting a known criminal. And as a bonus, my galumphing elephant of a dog had other, more innocent ways of torturing a man who happened to own a shop full of delicate things.

I strolled on into Something Old Something New with Plant at my side, the proverbial bull in a china shop, and waited for Earnest to start yelling at us. My plan was to point out that he was probably under police scrutiny now, and that he might not want to call the police or make a scene. Then I'd tell him I'd be happy to leave quietly, in exchange for five minutes of his time.

This plan thoroughly flopped.

Apparently Earnest just loved dogs. Plant was entirely and warmly welcomed into Something Old Something New.

But that was okay, since Plant also turned out to be my ticket in. Earnest, who was not wearing his sunglasses today, said he'd have kicked me out the second he saw my face, if I hadn't had that "adorable little guy" with me.

Adorable I could see. Little, not so much. But since Earnest was looking about a million times more cooperative already, I wasn't about to argue the point. He came around the counter and crouched down to pet Plant, who licked his new friend's chin and hands in return. (So much for a dog's natural instinct about people.)

"And the reason you would have kicked me out," I said, "would that have anything to do with the fact that the shelves you had all those fake dolls on are empty today?"

Earnest stood and pressed his hand to his chest. "I was shocked—*shocked*—to discover that the antique dolls I paid such a pretty price for were inauthentic." He shook his head sadly. "You can't trust anybody these days."

I crossed my arms. "Did the police buy that?"

He shrugged. "What do you want?"

"Same thing I wanted last time. Information."

Earnest snorted. "Why would I tell you anything?"

"Because you like my dog." I cocked my head, looking behind him. "And because those 'antique' maps you've got on the wall are fake, too. I'll bet I could find lots of fake stuff in here. How many times do you think claiming ignorance will get you out of trouble?"

He looked sulky, but didn't answer.

"Or," I said, "you could just answer one very simple question that will cost you nothing, and me and Plant here will be on our way, and it'll have turned out to be a very pleasant visit for you, what with having made a new dog buddy and all."

"Guess that depends on how simple that question is."

"All I want to know is whether after you made the fake knife—"

Earnest's eyes widened as he rushed to interrupt me. "I did no such thing! I already told you, I only deal in authentic antiquities. If I was taken advantage of by some unscrupulous dealer, I—"

"Yeah, yeah," I cut in. "Did you arrange a buyer?"

He blinked at me. "For what?"

I blinked back. "For the knife."

Earnest went on looking confused, and if it was an act, he was a much more talented actor than he was a forger. Which his overdramatic insistence that he'd never forged anything would seem to contradict. "If, hypothetically, someone asked me to render a service which I may or may not have allegedly rendered, why would they ask me to arrange a buyer? I mean, if I was going to make it and then just turn around and sell it, why would I need them?"

"Not for the fake one," I said. "The fake one was to replace a real one, so the owner wouldn't notice the difference."

Well, a real one, or a more believable fake one. It was still as improbable as ever that the Howells had possessed a real notation knife. But I didn't see the point in disparaging Earnest's workmanship by implying that a better forgery existed.

Earnest looked impressed. "If I'd made a knockoff knife, which of course I did not, I guess that would be a pretty smart plan."

"Yeah, well, it didn't work out. Did you find a buyer for the real one, or not?"

Earnest burst out laughing. "I guess you don't know much about these knives, huh?"

I tried not to look offended. "I know a bit."

"Then you should know they're priceless."

"Of course I do. But even priceless things end up having a price. That's—"

"Lady, look around." Earnest laughed again. "I sell dolls and maps and the occasional piece of jewelry. Do I look like the kind of guy who would have the sort of connections you'd need to offload a thing like that?"

Well, he certainly had a point there. The sort of private collector who could afford something as rare and valuable as a notation knife would not be hanging around Something Old Something New.

I'd just kind of figured the criminals knew the other criminals. Wouldn't he know where to find some sort of high-class art thievery ring? Didn't the forgers have an online forum or something?

Apparently not. I thanked Earnest for his time, let him give Plant a few parting pats, and turned to go.

A woman with a stroller was approaching the door just as Plant and I were exiting. I held it open for her and said in a low voice, "Avoid the maps."

"So how *do* you sell a thing like that?" I asked Plant as I took the Bryd Hollow exit off the highway.

Maybe Brooke was the one who knew a high-class art thievery ring. Percy had called her a globetrotter. She would meet all sorts of people, in a job like that.

All sorts, though? Whoever the buyer was, or would be, they wouldn't be just a little rich. They would have to be oil-magnate rich, or prince-of-a-small-country rich.

Odsbodikins, Minerva, why are you such a nitwit?

"Gosh, Plant." I gave him a pointed look in the rearview mirror, as if he'd been the one to miss the glaringly obvious. "Where would Ron and Brooke meet somebody like that?"

Plant thumped his tail, apparently interpreting this as me offering him a treat. Feeling generous now that I was sure I was on to something, I gave him one out of the stock I kept in the cupholder.

"I'll tell you where," I said as he chomped it. "The same place the citizens of Bryd Hollow meet all the rich people they know."

As soon as I got back to my desk, I called Lilian Berk, who was Tybryd's decorator and art buyer. I had no suspicions that the Digbys would try to sell the knife to *her*. They'd never be stupid enough to sell it to a local resident. But she often gave tours to guests and talked to them about the various pieces throughout the resort. She would know which of Tybryd's regular—or even irregular—visitors were collectors, aficionados, or dealers in rarities.

As I'd hoped, she gave me several names, although supplying a reason I would need such a list wasn't especially easy. The best I could come up with was that I was working on a potential artists' retreat, and if they ended up selecting Tybryd for the event, we might want to send out a mailing to a few select people who would be interested in meeting them.

"Isn't that a violation of the artists' privacy, though?" she wanted to know.

"No, no, it was their idea. One of the reasons they're looking at such swanky places to have it is so they can schmooze some potential buyers."

I figured while I was on a roll, I might as well not stop at lying to poor Lilian Berk. My next order of business was to conduct a slightly unethical and possibly illegal search of the hotel's database.

None of the names she'd given me had been guests in the past month. But one, a Mr. Stanley Glen, had a reservation that very weekend.

My pulse sped up. This might just be my buyer.

And if it was, then the Digbys hadn't sold the knife yet. Or at least, they hadn't delivered it.

I needed to find that knife—before it changed hands. If Brooke had it, surely Ron wouldn't let his own daughter go to jail for a crime he'd committed. And if Ron had it, well, I might never be able to prove Brooke's involvement, but at least the actual killer would be exposed.

Besides, it might give me a chance to see the real knife. So I could see if it was really a real knife. (Which of course it wasn't. It couldn't be. Right?)

But once the deal was done and the knife was gone, so was any connection between Ron Digby and Keith Howell's murder. Unless Ruby turned up some forensic evidence, but I couldn't count on that.

So I needed the knife. And not only that, but I needed to prove that it was in the Digbys' possession.

The best way to do both was to catch them in the act of making the exchange with Mr. Glen.

But how? I couldn't exactly bug a guest's room.

Could I?

I drummed my fingers against my desk, considering just how many crimes I was willing to commit, in the name of solving this one.

"Who would take care of you, if I went to jail?" I asked Plant.

Percy, probably.

Then I realized that wouldn't be necessary.

The Digbys could conduct their business in the privacy of Mr. Glen's room—but they wouldn't. Things were too hot in Bryd Hollow, now that Keith was dead. What should have been a simple steal and switch, with Keith none the wiser, had gotten a lot more complicated. They wouldn't want to risk being seen going into Stanley Glen's hotel room. They wouldn't want anybody connecting them with him at all.

No wonder Brooke hadn't told anybody the real reason for our fight. The last thing she needed now was the watchful gaze of Bryd Hollow's curious. A group that consisted of absolutely everybody in Bryd Hollow.

So where could she or Ron cross paths with an out-of-towner, without it looking like a planned meeting? Or better yet, without it looking like a meeting at all?

The answer to that was plain. I called the concierge desk.

"Hey, it's Minerva in events," I told the young voice that picked up. It wasn't one I recognized. A student, maybe, doing a short stint over spring break. So much the better. "I'm arranging a few things for Mr. Stanley's visit this weekend."

"Mr. Stanley's having an event?"

"No, but he's a VIP, so he gets a little extra. Can you tell me which nights he already has dinner reservations?"

It was a lame explanation, but the temp didn't know how things worked here, or if she did, she didn't care all that much. I heard the click of keys. "He's at Rapunzel's on Sunday at five-thirty."

"Thank you. Thank you very much." I hung up the phone, but only for a second.

Then I called Ruby Walker and invited her to dinner.

Chapter Twenty-Two

IF NOT FOR the fact that it was March, and Sunday, and early for dinner, I'd never have been able to get a reservation. I would have liked to invite Paul and Carrie too, Carrie being Ruby's niece, but a table for four on such short notice was out of the question.

That I did get a reservation was a source of excitement, not only for me, but for Ruby, who'd never sampled Bo Blue's famous food before, and on a cop's salary wasn't likely to get another chance.

I wasn't exactly dripping with money either, but the cost of the meal would be worth it if it meant catching the Digbys, thus making me look just a little bit less like a nitwit. Oh, and justice being served, and all that. Of course that was important, too.

By that time, I knew Ruby and her opinion of my crime-solving skills well enough to know exactly how this would go, if I was forthcoming with her about my motivation: she wouldn't half believe any of what I told her. I needed her to see it with her own eyes. The dinner invitation was the best plan I had.

Not that she was fooled by it. She and I had never had dinner together, and now I'd invited her, alone, to not only someplace expensive, but someplace owned by the family of the woman I'd already accused of Keith's murder. It didn't exactly take a fizzing investigator to work out that I was up to something.

"Are you going to make a scene?" she asked over the phone.

"Nope," I said, and hoped it was true.

"Are you going to harass Brooke Digby in any way?"

"Nope," I said again. And hoped that was also true.

"And are you going to do anything I might have to arrest you for?" Ruby asked.

"Nope." *Please let that be true.*

That had been enough for her to accept. Whatever I was up to, there was a free Bo Blue meal involved, and she was willing to play along.

I was anxious and fidgety as we walked in, for any number of reasons.

What if this was one of those things, like in psychic stories, where my knowing what was going to happen ended up changing what was going to happen? I might have needed Ruby there to see things go down, but there was also the chance that her presence would prevent things from going down. Ron wasn't about to whip out the knife in front of the police chief.

But maybe that was okay. After all, I didn't actually need him or his daughter to finish the deal. *Selling* the knife wasn't my proof that he'd killed Keith; *having* it was.

The reservation was in my name, which meant neither Ron nor Brooke would have any way of knowing Ruby would be at dinner until they saw her. Whether or not one of them actually made the exchange, one of them would have come prepared to. All I had to do was get them to show the knife.

How, I wasn't sure. The lump of nerves in my stomach suggested vomiting on one of them might somehow help.

Those nerves weren't eased any by the sight of Percy and Brooke, sitting by the window again, although at least this time it wasn't a romantic table for two. Bonnie was with them, and Paul and Carrie.

I guessed it was a good thing I hadn't made things awkward by inviting Paul and Carrie the same night. The traitors, why hadn't they told me they were having dinner with Percy and Brooke?

Maybe because they'd known I would use words like *traitors* if they did.

As soon as he saw me, Percy's jaw tightened. I was pretty sure it wasn't just that he was mad at me; he didn't like that I was there with Ruby. This theory was confirmed only seconds after we sat down, when Percy got up and walked over to our table, all dimples, like he was just saying hello to some friends. He greeted Ruby and kissed each of her cheeks, then leaned down to hug me.

He smelled really good. Naturally, I did not let this affect me in the least.

"Whatever you're up to," he hissed in my ear, "don't."

Great. He'd be watching me. Like I wasn't already anxious enough.

"So," Ruby said as she opened her menu. "You going to let me in on what this is about? Or just let whatever fool-headed plan you've got going on unfold?"

I bit my lip. Was there any point in denying I had a plan, fool-headed or otherwise? Probably not. "Unfold, if you don't mind."

"Can't wait."

Stanley Glen and his wife arrived just as our appetizers did. I knew it was them, because I'd done a social media search and found pictures. Why have any shame when it came to that, given all the other stalking I'd done?

Thankfully, I could see their table from ours. I didn't have a lot to say to Ruby, nor she to me, but that just gave me more time to watch the room. I kept an eye out for Ron, whom I hadn't seen yet.

And when I did see him, I would ... what? Just tackle Ron Digby in front of everybody and search his person for the knife?

I wished Plant were there; he'd have happily stolen it and pranced around the restaurant with it, and we'd have been able to call it a night. But alas.

Something would come to me. Some opportunity, some divine inspiration. The (probably not real, but supposedly real, and maybe even distantly possibly real) notation knife was in this building. I was so close. I was going to get my proof, one way or another.

While I stared at Stanley, Percy stared at me. This was not helping.

But at least I had a delectable duck breast, swimming in a buttery sour-cherry sauce, to console myself with. I took a blissful bite—then stopped halfway through chewing it.

Brooke knew I was on to them. Which probably meant Ron knew it. Were Bonnie and Bo involved, too? I still didn't know. I had no evidence that they were. But they *could* be.

That would put a whole lot of people in this restaurant who wished me ill—and one of them had cooked this duck.

Surely they wouldn't poison me while I was sitting with the police chief. They didn't even know how much I'd told her yet. It would be way too suspicious if I dropped dead on the floor at Rapunzel's, the very night they were supposed to offload the knife. Wouldn't it?

Of course it would. And anyway, no self-respecting chef would ever spoil a sauce this velvety and delicious with rat poison. It didn't taste anything like rat poison.

Scolding myself for being paranoid, I tried to swallow —but the damage was already done. My mouth had gone dry. The duck lodged itself in my throat.

I coughed. I sputtered. I stood and gasped and tried to gulp down some water, only to spill most of it down the front of my dress. Ruby got up and smacked my back. Percy materialized at my side.

I pushed him away—he was blocking my view of the Glens' table. I forced the duck down my throat at last, and wiped my watering eyes to find Ron Digby standing between Mr. Glen's chair, and Mrs. Glen's.

He must have come out during the commotion. How kind of me to make a scene and provide a distraction.

All three of them were staring at me. As were most of the other diners. I held up my shaking hand and did a little parade wave. "I'm fine. All good. Eating too fast. The food is really good, isn't it?"

Minerva, sit down and shut your nitwitted mouth.

My inner voice was a lot smarter than my outer one. I obeyed it. Percy went back to his own table (without a word to me, that I'd heard). Everybody else went back to their meals. The normal noise level resumed.

Ron started to walk away from the Glens' table, then turned back to Stanley, casually, as if it were an afterthought, and leaned down to say something near his ear. Stanley nodded, said something to his wife—and then followed Ron toward the back of the restaurant.

Were they going to do this now? In front of Ruby? Would Ron be that bold—or stupid? Maybe he would, now that I'd so helpfully drawn attention to myself.

No. This was a setup. He was trying to trap me into doing something nitwitted.

I wasn't going to fall for that.

Unless.

What if Stanley didn't know anything illegal was going on? What if he didn't know the knife had ever belonged to Keith Howell, or that Keith Howell was dead, or even that there *was* a Keith Howell?

How would he know? He didn't live here. He was

just an art dealer. And as far as I could tell, a legitimate one.

He probably had no idea the knife was stolen.

If he thought he was entering into a legitimate transaction, then Ron would have to act like it was a legitimate transaction. He couldn't tell Stanley the deal was off because the police chief was there.

The best Ron could do was invite Stanley into the back, while they had a gap between courses, to conduct their business. Ostensibly to get it out of the way, so Stanley and his wife could enjoy the rest of their evening.

And hope that if he did it quietly and quickly enough, nobody would catch him.

Well, I was going to catch him.

Unless I was wrong. In which case I was indeed about to make a supreme nitwit of myself.

Again.

Fine. If that was the worst that would happen, bring it on. I was getting used to it.

With a quick excuse to Ruby about going to the ladies' room to fix my makeup (which the choking incident would definitely have smudged, had I been wearing any), I set my napkin on the table and hurried after Ron. But not too fast. I knew where his office was.

Would he lock the door? Would that look weird to Stanley?

The door was closed. I heard voices inside. They were in there.

I tried the knob. It turned.

I walked into the room. Ron and Stanley both looked startled.

"Get out!" Ron barked.

"Oh gosh, I'm sorry," I said, wide-eyed. "I must have gotten turned around. Is this not the ladies' room?"

"You know it's not the ladies' room."

Drat. That was Percy's voice.

I turned to find him standing behind me, arms crossed. "What are you up to, Minerva?"

I had the fleeting thought that I kind of missed that *Mini Bigs* thing.

"I'd like to know that, too." Brooke came stalking up behind him. "It wasn't enough that you harassed me? Now you're harassing my father?"

"What is going on?" Stanley asked.

"I have the same question." Ruby pushed past Percy and Brooke, into the office. We would qualify as a crowd pretty soon.

She looked at me over the top of her glasses (again). "You are not wearing mascara. You didn't think I'd notice a thing like that? You didn't think I saw you watching him"—she gestured at Stanley—"like a hawk all night?"

I shrugged. I didn't mind that I'd been obvious. Not to her, anyway. I'd have preferred not to have Brooke and Percy there, sure, but Ruby's presence was only going to make this easier.

Because Ron Digby had gone pale.

And Stanley Glen had *not.*

Stanley only looked confused. Or so I thought. Not that I knew him well. Or at all.

I was going to have to risk everything on one roll of the dice, based on my interpretation of the expression of a man I'd never seen in person. Sure. What could go wrong?

It wasn't like I'd been humiliated before, while insisting I'd solved this particular crime.

Stanley asked again what was going on. Bonnie showed up to ask the same. There was that crowd, then. So much for not making a scene.

Everybody was looking at me. I took a deep breath.

"What's going on," I said, "is that the knife Ron is selling you is stolen property, Mr. Glen. Were you aware of that?"

One of two things was going to happen next: Either I was wrong, and Stanley Glen was entirely complicit in what Ron Digby was doing, and would deny that he was buying anything at all. Which would be bad. Really *really* bad.

Or else I was right, and Stanley Glen was an honest man. One who would be shocked to find that the piece he was about to buy was connected to theft and murder. One who would want no part in such dastardly deeds, and would immediately express his indignation and cooperate with the policewoman in the room.

I held my breath as I waited for Stanley to react, wishing and praying for option two.

"What are you talking about?" Stanley looked from me to Ron. "What is she talking about?"

So he was playing ignorant about the sale. My heart sank.

"I haven't the slightest idea," said Ron. "Minerva, and everyone else, I'm afraid I'm going to have to ask you to leave. Yes, even you, Bonnie. Get back to your meals.

Mr. and Mrs. Glen's entrees will be arriving soon, and Mrs. Glen is out there alone, so we really don't have time to—"

"You told me the notation knife had been passed down through your family for generations," Stanley cut in.

My heart leapt back up again. Everybody stared at Ron. Even Ruby looked shocked.

Brooke did not.

"It was passed down through *a* family," I said. "Just not his. He stole it. And by the way, killed its owner while he was at it." I looked at Ruby, but jerked my head at Brooke. "She was in on it, too."

"What?" Brooke and Ron both asked the question at the same time.

I rolled my eyes at Brooke. "Oh, come on. You pumped Dottie for information about the knife. You went to Something Old Something New to—"

I stopped abruptly. *To what?*

Earnest hadn't arranged a buyer, or according to him, even offered to try. And by the time Brooke went to Something Old Something New, Ron already had the counterfeit knife. There was no reason for Brooke to have been there that day.

Unless ...

Even as I was having these thoughts, Ron seemed to confirm them. "You went to Something Old Something New?" he asked his daughter. "When? Why?"

Odsbodikins.

I'd noticed Earnest using the word *they*: why would *they* ask me to arrange a buyer, why would I need *them*.

I'd assumed it was plural *they*—because I'd been thinking in those terms.

But he was just being coy about the gender of his client.

Brooke crossed her arms. "Because I wanted to know what you were up to, Dad." She glared at me. "Obviously."

Drat and double drat. So she'd stumbled onto some part of Ron's plan—a message, a phone number, maybe even the fake knife—and set about investigating the rest.

She'd been following the same trail I was; she'd just done it sooner. Unfortunately for Keith Howell, not soon enough.

Brooke Digby was innocent.

And I was a nitwit. Again.

"What *were* you up to, Dad?" Bonnie wailed. "What did you do?"

That seemed to open the floodgates. Everybody started talking—or in some cases, yelling—at once. Ruby spoke to Stanley. Bonnie screamed at her father. Ron bellowed back, insisting he hadn't stolen anything that didn't by rights belong to the Digbys. Brooke scolded both her sister and her father. Percy scolded Brooke, demanding to know what she'd known, and when. She didn't answer him; I wasn't sure she heard him.

I was the only one who was quiet. I was pretty much out of things to say.

"Enough!" Ron stepped back from the fray, hands on the sides of his head as if he couldn't take the noise anymore. He looked around, at his daughters, at Ruby, at Stanley. His lips trembled, opened, closed again.

Finally his eyes rested on me. They were not looking friendly.

Then he lunged at me.

His arms were outstretched, and heading fast in the general direction of my throat.

I was prepared to defend myself with a well-placed kick, but I never got the chance. Percy's fist connected with my would-be strangler's jaw, and Ron Digby went down.

"Where is it?" Ruby stood over him, hands on her hips. It was an excellent angle from which to give him The Glasses Of Disapproval.

The punch seemed to have knocked the wind out of Ron's sails. Looking utterly defeated, and maybe even a little teary, he reached into his jacket and produced a padded envelope.

Ruby took it, opened it, and pulled out what was inside.

And I got, at long last, my first look at the (supposedly) real notation knife. One that had (supposedly) belonged to Anne Boleyn, and then Henry VIII, before passing to Tudor descendants of less and less prominence, until it ended up in the Howell family.

While all the while, the Boleyn line went on too, through Mary. Until a branch by the name of Digby moved to Bryd Hollow.

And the rest, as they say, is history.

Chapter Twenty-Three

"So Ron was strapped for cash, found out about the knife—do we know how or when he found out?" Percy hopped down a particularly rocky dip in the hiking trail, then turned around to offer me his hand.

I took it, but as soon as I was past the rough ground I said, "It's okay, you know, I don't need help."

He kept hold of my hand for just a tiny bit longer than necessary. "I know. But maybe I need to help."

My heart did a little somersault, which I pretended to ignore. "Fair enough. And no, we don't know how Ron found out about the knife, but he could have known for ages, and only gotten the details recently. It would've been the song that tipped him off. Once he found out there was a song from Anne's songbook on a knife of Henry's, he decided that knife belonged to his family."

I called for Plant, who was too far ahead now for me to see. He came bounding back, poked first me and then Percy with his nose, then ran ahead again. Off-leash trails were a rare treat for him, and he couldn't contain his excitement. Probably because he made no effort to contain his excitement.

"Or maybe he knew all along," Percy said. "Maybe they've known since Molly Towe, but Ron didn't do anything about it until he got desperate." He shook his head. "I don't get how they could hold onto this Henry-Anne thing for four hundred years, or whatever it is."

"Almost five hundred," I said. "And really? You don't get it? Let me tell you about a little town called Bryd Hollow."

Percy snickered. "I guess it helps if the feud conveniently means you get to take something super valuable at a time when you really, really need money."

"Speaking of Molly Towe," I said, "I have some news on that front. I got an email from Tracey Howell a couple days ago. She'd just had an ultrasound. The baby's a girl."

"So maybe the spell was on the knife, and now that it's gone, so's the curse."

I spread my hands. "Or maybe the whole thing was a lot of coincidence."

"That does seem likelier, but a curse is more fun."

I couldn't argue with that. The curse had captured my imagination, too, and a part of me liked the thought of Anne's restless spirit finding some amusement in taking her knife away from Henry's people.

Not that I thought that was a good reason for Keith Howell to die. But I doubted his death would have given either the Tudors or the Boleyns any pause. Both had been brutal families.

Percy pushed aside a branch so I could walk under it.

"What if the knife was actually Molly Towe's idea? Purely so she could curse it and give it to the Howells."

"You're suggesting Molly Towe forged the knife? Like some sort of bait?"

"Kind of." He hit me with the full force of his dimples. I won't deny it made me a little breathless. I'd gone too long without them. "You want to know why I asked you on this hike?"

"I thought it was an excuse to bring us cupcakes and dog treats and beg my forgiveness."

Which was what he'd done. And which was pretty nice of him, considering he had not, technically, been wrong about Brooke. Said forgiveness was freely and immediately granted; the cupcakes were amazing. (Tea would have done the job just fine, but I didn't tell him that.)

"Well, that," he said, "and also—"

"My dazzling company and witty conversation?"

"That too, but I wanted to tell you the real kicker. I just found out this morning."

"Found out what?"

"The real knife isn't real either. It's just a better fake."

I whistled softly. It had been a week since Ron Digby was arrested for the murder of Keith Howell. Long enough for him to confess and, I heard, make a deal with the DA, since the murder part was an accident.

Long enough for Brooke to leave town, after Ruby decided not to charge her with anything.

Long enough for Bonnie and Bo Blue to quietly elope, her dreams of a big Tybryd wedding having been soured by the scandal. I still didn't like her, but I did feel bad for her.

But was a week really long enough to authenticate—or not—the knife? "Are they sure?"

"Sounds like it."

We caught up to Plant, who was sniffing around an old tree stump, and I stopped to scratch his head. It had always been unlikely that the Howell family just happened to have a notation knife, that that knife had ever belonged to an English king, that it would have a secular song on it, and that that song would be Anne Boleyn's. The whole thing stretched credibility well beyond its limits. I knew this.

But still. Ruby had let me hold it, for a few seconds, before she took it away.

"You look sad," said Percy.

I shrugged. "I would've loved to be able to say I held something that belonged to Anne Boleyn. And a real actual notation knife, no less."

He squeezed my hand. "Would another apology cheer you up? Because I had at least three planned out."

"Were they all going to involve baked goods?"

"Obviously. Think I'm fool enough to go with flowers? I know the way to your heart."

Do you?

Seeming to realize what he'd just said, Percy dropped my hand and scratched the back of his neck. "Anyway. I should have known better than to take Brooke's side over yours."

I shook my head. "You two have a lot of history. She has a better claim to your loyalty than I do."

"No," he said quietly. "She doesn't."

It was my turn to squeeze his hand. "I'm sorry. It must have been hard to lose her again."

I'd heard from Paul, who heard from Carrie, who heard from Bonnie, that Percy and Brooke had had quite a spat before she left town, and would not be staying in touch.

It didn't surprise me. She'd sleuthed out the identity of Keith's murderer just as much as I had—and she'd been trying to cover it up. I was sure Percy understood, what with it being her own father and all, but even so. Nobody that dishonest would have long-term potential for him. He was an honorable man.

But he shrugged off my condolences as he turned away. "Eh, we mostly talked about you."

I grabbed his elbow to stop him walking. "What do you mean, about me?" I narrowed my eyes at him. "Percy Baird, were you trying to make me jealous?"

"No! I'm not ... I wouldn't play games like that!" He kicked at the dirt, eyes down. "I'll confess I wouldn't have *objected* to you being jealous. But that wasn't the point. I was catching up with an old friend. We talked about you a lot because I ..." He tossed a hand. "... talk about you a lot."

"Do you." I stepped closer to him. For the first time since I'd met him, and possibly ever, Percy Baird went still.

I'd had enough of all this hemming and hawing and vague back-and-forth between us. It was time for us to decide how we felt. And then come clean about it.

Him first, though.

"And why is that?" I pressed.

He didn't answer, but he did try to kiss me.

I say *tried* not because I stopped him, which I certainly and totally did not, but because Plant got kind of excited about us getting close together, like he wanted in on any group hug that might be happening. He pushed himself into the way, and tripped me, and then Percy kind of tripped when he tried to catch me, and it was all very ungraceful and, considering the dog slobber, not all that romantic.

But it was still pretty great.

Dear Reader

Thank you for reading *Old Knives Tale*. I hope you enjoyed it! Minerva's next adventure is *Past Resort*.

If you'd like to know when I've got a new book, be sure to sign up for my newsletter at cordeliarook.com. You'll find my email address there as well; I love to hear from readers!

Your honest ratings and reviews help other readers choose books. I hope you'll consider giving your opinion at your online retailer.

Minervaisms

butter upon bacon: even more of a good thing; over the top; an extravagance

carriwitchet: a befuddling question; a puzzle

fizzing: excellent; impressive

hornswaggler: a fraud or cheat

nanty-narking: having great fun; partying

odsbodikins: an all-purpose expression of dismay, surprise, or irritation, similar to "Oh my gosh!" or "Gosh darnit!"

pantry politicking: gossiping among the household, staff, or servants

podsnappery: a refusal to recognize the unpleasant; complacency

ratbag: a jerk; a sleazy person

Made in United States
North Haven, CT
04 May 2023

36212679R10139